W9-ALN-609

WHISKEY CREEK

Also by Gary McCarthy

The First Sheriff
Winds of Gold
The Legend of the Lone Ranger
Silver Winds
Wind River
Powder River
The Last Buffalo Hunt
Mando
The Mustangers
Transcontinental
Sodbuster
Blood Brothers
The Colorado River
The Russian River
The Gringo Amigo
The American River

Derby Man Books

The Derby Man
Showdown at Snakegrass Junction
Mustang Fever
The Pony Express War
Silver Shot
Explosion at Donner Pass
North Chase
Rebel of Bodie
The Rail Warriors

Gary McCarthy

WHISKEY CREEK

A DOUBLE D WESTERN

DOUBLEDAY

New York London Toronto Sydney Auckland

A Double D Western
PUBLISHED BY DOUBLEDAY
a division of Bantam Doubleday Dell Publishing Group, Inc.
666 Fifth Avenue, New York, New York 10103

DOUBLE D WESTERN, DOUBLEDAY
and the portrayal of the letters DD
are trademarks of Doubleday, a division of
Bantam Doubleday Dell Publishing Group, Inc.

All of the characters in this book are fictitious
and any resemblance to actual persons, living or
dead, is purely coincidental.

Library of Congress Cataloging-in-Publication Data

McCarthy, Gary.
Whiskey Creek/Gary McCarthy.—1st ed.
p. cm.—(A Double D Western)
I. Title.
PS3563.C3373W47 1992
813′.54—dc20 91-44040
CIP

ISBN 0-385-41989-9

Printed in the United States of America
July 1992
First Edition

For Beverly Eastland:
Kemo Sabe, trusted friend

WHISKEY CREEK

ONE

"BLAST!" Darby hissed as he slumped down in the seat of the Central Pacific Railroad car bound for Reno, Nevada. "Blast it, anyway!"

Several of the other passengers glanced over at the famed Derby Man, but when he turned his angry gaze back on them, they quickly looked away. Two cars ahead, there was a private coach with a band and all the free liquor a man could stomach just for the asking; but Darby was in no mood to celebrate the completion of the transcontinental railroad, in spite of the fact that he had been instrumental in its victorious union at Promontory Point, Utah.

Grumbling still, Darby pulled an expensive Cuban cigar out of his coat pocket, savagely lopped off its tip with a silver pen knife and absently placed it in his mouth. Then he not only forgot to light the cigar but actually whipped his head around toward the window and drove the cigar halfway down his throat before it snapped.

"Ahhheh!" he choked, finally managing to clear his throat. Confound it, he thought, I can't do anything right! My mind has completely taken its leave.

He brushed the shreds of tobacco from his tailor-made black frock coat, feeling humiliated. It depressed him to realize that, as long as Dolly was missing, he undoubtedly would continue to make a fool of himself.

Where was she! And why, after all the years of pursuing matrimony, had the sensuous Miss Beavers mysteriously failed to meet him at Promontory Point for their nuptials? Their wedding had been anticipated by the national press almost as much as the completion of the transcontinental railroad itself.

Darby wondered again—had Dolly forsaken him for a younger, handsomer man? Darby's mind recoiled at the possibility and yet he knew Dolly was capable of attracting any man. She was a stunning and highly passionate woman. She had deep blue eyes, long blonde hair and the body of a love goddess.

"She could have any man," he muttered, "any man she wants."

Perversely, Darby studied his own face in the window's grimy reflection. His fist-busted nose was bent and he was scarred a little about the eyes, but remarkably little, considering the hundreds of prizefights he'd won while holding the title of America's bareknuckle champion. Glorious years, those, but they did leave a man with a few physical reminders.

Still, he was sure that Dolly had loved his face despite its flaws. And he was not a man without some attractive qualities. To begin with, he was rather well-to-do—not rich, but certainly comfortably fixed, thanks to his wise investments and his success as America's leading dime novelist. Also, he was a gourmet, a connoisseur of fine wines, and considered rather charming and generous by men and women alike. In truth, women had always been attracted to him, especially during the time when he'd been a circus strongman in black tights. Oh, those had been heady days! He had lifted weights that astonished even his peers.

But in spite of all those fine attributes of his, Dolly *was* missing. It was a worry and a mystery, and as he pondered it once again Darby took out another cigar, this time being careful not to twist his head and jam the damn thing down his throat. He puffed rapidly enough to envelop himself in a cloud of thick black smoke. Sinking even deeper into his seat, he closed his eyes, wondering if Dolly had fallen ill. Or, God forbid, even expired. Darby shuddered and consoled himself by remembering that, like himself, she had always enjoyed perfect health.

"Maybe she's fallen victim to some foul play," he mused aloud.

Darby puffed faster. It was no secret that he was a man of means. Therefore, it was reasonable to conclude that Dolly was a candidate for kidnapping for ransom. If that were the case, all Darby had to do was return to Reno, await the expected ransom demand and then extract Dolly from her abductors and seek retribution. It seemed simple enough, but the idea of Miss Dolly Beavers being held hostage and perhaps compromised was almost unbearable.

"Mr. Buckingham, may I speak with you, sir?"

"Leave me in peace," Darby growled without turning his face from the window. He irritably crushed his cigar out under his heel. "I am unfit company."

"But, sir!"

Darby glanced up to see a tall, slender young man wearing a black suit, white shirt, black tie and derby hat exactly like his own. All were of the highest quality. One look told Darby that this was a rich young fellow, probably educated in some foppish Ivy League college.

"Go away, young man."

"I cannot. You see, Mr. Buckingham, I consider my entire future to be in your good hands."

Darby's brow furrowed. "Don't be absurd. Who are you?"

In reply, the young man reached inside his coat and drew out a very expensive calling card printed on the finest stock. "My name is Austin Applegate, Esquire."

Darby barely glanced at the card. "The name means nothing to me. What are you?"

Applegate drew in a long breath and paused dramatically before he said, "Mr. Buckingham, I am the man who intends to become your successor."

"What!"

"Yes, sir!" Austin Applegate announced with supreme confidence. "If you and God are willing, I mean to follow right in your footsteps and become your successor to fame and fortune."

Darby groaned. "I cannot answer for God but, for myself, if you don't exit this car immediately I will scoop you up and hurl you from this train."

Applegate paled but managed to stand his ground. "But, sir, I have excellent credentials! I was the editor of my university paper. I write poetry and prose equally well. And I seek—as you did, not so very long ago—adventure in the West. I don't ask for a byline and I'd never attempt to imitate your unique and famous writing style, but I do wish to learn from you." He flashed a tight, quick smile. "As you can see, I've even adopted your wardrobe, right down to my rather out-of-date round-toed shoes."

"They're not out-of-date and you had better get lost, Mr. Applegate."

"But, Mr. Buckingham, I've read every word you've ever written! Can't you see that you are my hero? After all, I could have read great writers and studied classic tales but, instead, I chose to emulate *you!*"

Darby wasn't sure whether he had been flattered or insulted. Probably the latter. Still, there was no denying that the lad was extremely earnest.

"Listen," Darby said, wanting to be reasonable, "I am honored by your interest in my life and my dime novels, but right now I am very, very preoccupied."

"Of course you are! Who wouldn't be, with Miss Beavers disappearing without even a word of explanation. Take heart! I will help, no matter what evil circumstances may have befallen her."

"What makes you think that she's in trouble?"

Austin cleared his throat. "Why else would any reasonable and intelligent woman forsake you?"

"I agree and confess that her disappearance baffles me exceedingly," Darby said, "but that does not alter the fact that I've given the conductor orders that I am not to be disturbed."

"Mr. Buckingham, I understand completely, because I know how newspaper and tabloid reporters can offend a man of your refined sensibilities."

Austin plunked down beside the Derby Man. He drew a Cuban cigar from his coat pocket and it was Darby's own brand. "Smoke?"

"Why, thank you."

"My pleasure." Austin lit their cigars. "I saw all those reporters flocking about you at Promontory Point like buzzards after decaying carrion. They'd sell their mothers and their souls for an interview, then distort the truth every way imaginable in order to sell their despicable copy."

Darby's chin dipped in agreement. "Agreed."

Austin blew a big smoke ring up the aisle. "The thing of it is, Mr. Buckingham, that kind of writer lacks both talent and sensitivity. They will never understand the artist's mind."

"Oh, hogwash!" Darby exploded. "Now get out of here before I hurl you through this window!"

"But . . ."

"Out!"

Applegate jumped so high that he banged his head on the overhead luggage rack, smashing his derby flat and stunning himself. He collapsed in the seat, eyelids quivering.

Darby took pity on the conceited young fool. Austin, despite his fine clothes, words and flattery, was human after all. "I trust you have not brained yourself, Mr. Applegate."

"No," Austin wheezed, "not entirely. But I've compressed a few vertebrae in my neck and I'll wager I'll soon have a splitting headache."

Darby reached inside his coat and retrieved a silver flask purchased in New York City. It was quite distinctive with its ivory cap and engraved silverwork. "Here."

Austin fumbled in his own coat pocket and retrieved an identical flask. "Thanks, but I have my own."

"What," Darby asked, sure that he already knew the answer, "are you drinking?"

"Why, your favorite—Roquet's French Brandy, of course."

Darby's thick brow knitted. "Of course. How much do you *really* know about me?"

"Everything that has ever been written."

When this admission evoked no response, Austin said, "Mr. Buckingham?"

"What?"

"If something evil has happened to Miss Beavers, even a man like you could stand some help. And I am not as helpless as I may appear. I've been tested by adversity and not found wanting."

Darby studied Austin's hands, then his handsome, boyish face. He did not see even one scar. "You've led a sheltered existence, Mr. Applegate. Don't deny it."

"But . . ."

"And," Darby said, overriding his objections, "it's obvious to me that you have never had a bad street-fight. You've never known real hardship or poverty, nor have you been in a life-or-death emergency, now have you?"

"Well, I admit that I . . ."

"So, I am right," Darby said. "It takes no great perception to see that you were born to privilege and wealth, unlike myself, who came up from the streets with nothing but a pair of rock-hard fists and muscle to earn my way to the top."

"All right!" the young man cried. "I *have* had it easy. I know you are a self-made man and I intend to become the same. I've informed my father that I don't want to inherit his factories or his money."

Darby blinked. "No!"

"Yes! I will make my own way in the West. I won't take a cent from my father's estate. I'll send his money right back. I've cut the ties, Mr. Buckingham. My father knows the path I have set my eyes upon. He knows that I admire you more than him, and that I will be nothing if not America's next great dime novelist."

Darby groaned. He shook his head. "Perhaps you and I had better spend a little time together," he said. "I think you might have a rather glorified idea of what it means to earn your living writing dime novels and chasing about the West in search of adventures."

"But I *do* know what it means! I've read everything you've written. It sounds wonderful. Even the hard and dangerous times. I can hardly wait to go hungry, sleep on rocks, go without water for days, ride an outlaw stallion and whip a roomful of men with my own bare knuckles."

Darby sighed. Enthusiasm was the greatest gift of all because, with it, a man could do things beyond his ordinary capabilities. But in Austin's case, enthusiasm had to be linked with realism.

"Listen, young man. All those things that I've written, well, I have been honest but I have also given the accounts a patina, a glow of excitement and adventure, that was not always present. There have been many times when I wished I was back in New York City leading a very luxurious existence."

"Oh, I understand that very well."

"You do?"

"Of course! But the thing of it is, Mr. Buckingham, despite the hardship and the sacrifices, you've remained out West, never once going back to the easy life of New York society. Isn't that so?"

"Yes, but . . ."

"And you love the West so much you now feel a part of it. Its sense of freedom and adventure has fired your soul

—at least that's what you claimed in *Rails West,* your latest dime novel. Isn't that so?"

"It is, but . . ."

"Then how can you deny me the opportunity to experience those same heady feelings of awe and wonder?" Austin grabbed his sleeve. "Mr. Buckingham, I know what you're thinking when you look at me."

"How could . . ."

"You're thinking that I look too frail, too weak to survive the adventures we shall encounter. But you're wrong! I've studied the art of fisticuffs and gone a round or two. And I am a marksman with a pistol—something which, by every account, you are not."

It was true. Darby was a terrible shot but to hear it from another rankled. "You forget that a double-barreled shotgun requires no great accuracy."

"Yes, but we both carry pearl-handled derringers in our vest pockets and I'll wager I can outshoot you every time. And there is something else."

"What?" Darby snapped.

"I'm a fine equestrian."

"Equestrian?" Darby's anger flashed. "You use that word out in this country and the cowboys will laugh you out of the room. There are no 'equestrians' on the range, Mr. Applegate! There are horsemen, broncbusters, cowboys and vaqueros. They all ride like men born to a saddle."

Austin's cheeks flamed but he managed to get his own temper under control. "I suppose I have shown my ignorance already," he said. "But given your almost legendary dislike for riding, I just thought . . ."

"Never mind," Darby said, cutting the man off. "I *am* poor with both gun and horse. But it takes other characteristics to survive out in this rough frontier country."

"I'll stand the test," Austin vowed. "I ask only for a chance."

Darby shook his head. "If Miss Beavers is really in trouble, I'll need to focus all my energy and concentration on rescuing her. I can't be worrying about your safety, too."

"I understand. I told my father the very same thing."

"And he said?"

"He said that I was insane to want to be a mere dime novelist like you when I could inherit his industrial empire. He thought me confused and disturbed—in need of expensive medical care. We parted on a rather bad note."

" 'Mere dime novelist'! Is that what he really called me?"

"Yes."

Darby's walruslike mustache twitched with irritation. "I take it he's never actually read anything I've written!"

"Of course not."

Darby relaxed. "Never mind your father. What about your mother?"

"She died when I was quite young, just as yours did, Mr. Buckingham. I hardly knew the poor woman yet have always keenly felt her presence."

That answer well suited the Derby Man for he felt the same way. And in spite of his better judgment, he rather admired the young dandy. After all, Austin had to be dedicated to his stated purpose of becoming a great dime novelist if he was turning his back on the family fortune. That showed character.

"What, exactly, would you write if I allowed you to accompany me on this mystery trail, wherever it might lead?"

"I want to chronicle it, of course."

"And what makes you think I wouldn't care to do the same?"

"Because it's too personal," Austin said without the slightest hesitation. "You can't possibly write about something so close to your heart as the disappearance of Miss Beavers."

Darby had to admit the young man was correct. "I'll tell you what," he said, "if this works out happily then I'll give you permission to write the account and have it published. But if it does not . . ."

"Then it will be a matter of honor and our secret," Austin said, looking Darby right in the eye.

"Very well then." Darby extended his hand, using a grip powerful enough to crush walnuts. "But if you betray my trust, you will long rue this day, Mr. Applegate."

"I understand completely," Austin said, trying to extract his hand from Darby's crushing grip. "But would you mind if I at least take notes from this point forward?"

"I suppose not."

Austin extracted a silver pen and a blue, leather-bound writing pad from his coat and began his notes. Darby did not wish to appear too curious so he chose to ignore the scratching of pen on paper. Still, he could not help but wonder what the young man was saying about him and he supposed it would be very complimentary.

"Mr. Buckingham, would you mind telling me how you reached the conclusion that Miss Dolly has been kidnapped for ransom?"

Darby thumbed back his derby and reached into his pocket for another Cuban cigar. "Like you, I could see no other reason why Miss Beavers would forsake me, except for death or grave illness."

Austin nodded in enthusiastic agreement and all the rest of that day they were engaged in conversation about the West and Darby's earlier grand adventures. Darby talked for hours about his role with the Pony Express and the assault of the Chinese tracklayers on the Sierra Nevada Mountains. He spoke of boom towns he'd visited such as the infamous Bodie, California, self-proclaimed "Baddest Town in the West."

"It's changing fast," Darby said with a sigh of regret. "Here and there you'll see barbed wire, and this transcontinental railroad is going to be the final nail in the coffin of the free-running buffalo herds."

"Then why did you work so hard to see it completed?"

"The country needed to be linked by rail," Darby said. "And it would be pretentious and foolish of me to think that I could hold back the western march for even one instant. No, change is coming to the West whether we want it or not."

"I hope I'm not too late to see the wild frontier and write about it," Austin fretted.

"You aren't. Oh, you missed a few historic things, but there is still more than a lifetime of wild times to see and live. It's dangerous and unpredictable, and in many parts of the West the only law is still a man's fist, knife or gun."

Austin brightened. "I can hardly wait!"

"The West keeps a man's instincts sharp because of its dangers," Darby warned.

"You do appear to be in your prime, sir, the picture of health."

"I am," Darby said proudly. "Oh, I have a few aches, and the joints in these fighter's hands of mine can be stiff and painful on cold days, but otherwise I feel very fit."

"There is some controversy about the precise reason you chose to come to the West and how soon it was that you met Miss Dolly Beavers. Could you clear that up?"

"Certainly. As my publisher, J. Franklin Warner, well recalls, I refused to write any more fabricated dime novels and insisted on journeying west to research and chronicle *real* stories. I met Miss Beavers soon after my arrival in Running Springs, Wyoming. She owned the Antelope Hotel and we enjoyed a mutual attraction."

"I see. What were the happy circumstances that brought you to that small Wyoming town?"

"I was researching a story on the famed lawman Zeb Cather. At the time, I was unknown in the West and, since I refused to wear the local garb, I was the object of some ridicule. Miss Beavers was . . . well, a little more understanding."

"I can't imagine anyone causing you any unpleasantness."

"Ah, but they did," Darby said. "This is my fourth or fifth derby hat. I've had them shot off my head and smashed down flat against my skull. In fights, I've often felt that my opponents are as interested in destroying my derby as they are in besting me!" Darby glanced up at the flattened derby resting on Austin Applegate's head. "I'd better warn you of the same."

Austin mustered up his courage. "If they do, I will teach them their manners."

"I see." Darby considered it a waste of breath to advise the young man that he would not have a chance in a Western saloon fight. Out here, there were no Marquis of Queensbury rules. It was smash, gouge and bite.

While Austin Applegate scribbled away, Darby turned back to the window and was delighted to see a band of wild mustangs about a mile away. The stallion, a big sorrel, danced in proud defiance and bugled a challenge as the smokey train chugged past.

"I wish," Darby said, "that this confounded train would pick up more speed. I'm very anxious about Miss Beavers."

Austin Applegate nodded with understanding, and their conversation continued until early evening when they both retired to the special coach that had been reserved for the Central Pacific dignitaries and their friends. Darby introduced Austin around and was surprised to learn that the Applegate family was quite well known. It transpired that the elder Mr. Applegate owned a foundry that had made rails for the North during the Civil War. Austin charmed his hosts and was obviously witty and intelligent. But could he write? And would the wealthy young man prove himself in a crisis?

These were questions of vital importance, and while Miss Beavers's safety was of the utmost concern, Darby knew that he would hold himself personally responsible should this young man come to a sad end.

Through the talk and the laughter, the tinkling of champagne bottles against lead crystal glasses in the elegant traveling car, Darby heard the locomotive's steam whistle begin to shriek as night fell on western Nevada. Stepping a little apart from the others, he recalled the magnificent feast that he and Dolly had shared on their last night in Reno—roasted pheasant under glass, sautéed veal, poached salmon, delicately seasoned fresh vegetables and, for dessert, strawberries swimming in cream, and all of it washed down with the finest French champagne that the Central Pacific's money could buy. Afterward, he had at long last proposed marriage.

The memory of that night caused Darby's eyes to sting and his throat to ache. If Dolly was dead, his heart would be shattered. Even now he fancied he could smell her cheap, overpowering perfume. And then he remembered something else about that night: while crossing the Virginia Street Bridge over the Truckee River, Dolly had been overwhelmed by a sudden premonition that something awful would come between them. Like a fool, he'd made light of her woman's fears.

Had she known even then of some looming danger? Darby thought so now and was filled with bitterness and regret. If only he'd listened to her! Perhaps she had wanted to tell him something of vital importance but he had been too dense to notice.

"Mr. Buckingham?"

Darby jerked his mind back from the past. He scrubbed his eyes dry to see young Austin looking at him with great concern. "Yes, Mr. Applegate?"

"We'll find her and she'll be all right."

Darby patted the young man's arm, genuinely touched. "If she's alive, I'll marry her yet, Mr. Applegate. And you shall be my best man."

Austin Applegate's chin lifted and he could not speak.

Darby turned away. At that moment, he wanted a cigar but he feared his hands would tremble while holding a match.

Yes, he vowed silently, if my Dolly is yet alive, we will find her!

TWO

IT WAS DARK by the time the train arrived in Reno. A cold March wind was blowing off the snow-capped Sierras and the heavens sparkled with frozen stars. Consumed by worry, the Derby Man fled the train station carrying two huge valises.

"Where are we going!" Austin cried, struggling to keep up and failing in spite of his youth and long legs.

"To the Riverfront Hotel," Darby shouted as they strode down Virginia Street toward the bridge over the Truckee River. The river, now fed by melting Sierra snow, was running almost full. The same ducks that Dolly had so loved to feed were now asleep on the riverbank. Every sight and smell reminded Darby of his beloved Dolly and of how much he missed and needed her.

The Riverfront Hotel was the finest establishment in Reno, two stories of red brick with an elegant lobby illuminated by two magnificent crystal chandeliers. The floors were checkered Italian marble, polished to a shine. Darby didn't notice any of this as he rushed across the lobby and dropped the luggage with a huge *thump.* He stomped his heels with impatience.

The hotel clerk appeared an instant later. At the sight of the Derby Man, he exclaimed, "Mr. Buckingham, what a wonderful surprise!"

"What happened to Miss Dolly Beavers? Is she still registered here?"

Darby looked so upset and menacing that the hotel clerk stammered, "Ahhh . . . I'm afraid not."

"Then where is she!"

"Mr. Buckingham, I don't know! She's just gone. She checked out last month with no explanation or forwarding address."

"Blast!" Darby struggled to regain his composure. "But . . . but surely you can tell me something of value."

The man reached under the desk and found a silver flask. He uncapped it and silently offered a drink to the Derby Man, who shook his head. The clerk drank enough for both of them. Courage fortified, he wiped his lips and said, "I can tell you that Miss Beavers was very upset when she left. I must also tell you that she was with a man."

Darby blanched. His mustache twitched and his black eyes flashed. His fingernails bit into the desk.

Austin, fearing that Darby would explode in a rage, quickly said, "Mr. Buckingham, it doesn't necessarily mean that she threw you over for someone else."

"Of course not!" Darby glared at the clerk. "Tell me every last detail about this man. Leave nothing to my rich imagination."

"Well, Mr. Buckingham, he just arrived one morning and stayed."

"Stayed!"

"Only until Miss Beavers checked out of this hotel, that very same afternoon."

"Describe him."

"He was tall, as tall as your friend, and I'd judge him to be in his late thirties. He had a cleft chin and I suppose women would judge him handsome. His face was weatherburned."

"Deeply tanned?"

"No. He had pale red hair and his face was burned."

"What about his physique? Was he slender like Mr. Applegate or more robust like myself?"

"Somewhat in between. I'd describe him as appearing very fit. He seemed to be the kind of man accustomed to giving orders and to having them followed."

"And his dress? A business suit? Working clothes? What?"

"He wore cowboy boots."

"Almost everyone wears them."

"Yes, but his were very expensive. Not black, but a soft tan color. He dressed like a successful cattle rancher. I'd say he definitely had money. He was no thirty-dollar-a-month cowboy, that's for sure. He wore a gold and turquoise ring. Never saw turquoise set in gold before. Indians always do it in silver. I remarked on that ring."

"And he said?"

"He said that gold and turquoise had been used together for centuries, right back to the Egyptians."

"Hmmm." Darby was starting to get a mental picture of the man but there were still big gaps. "What else can you tell me?"

"Well, like I said, he had pale red hair, sort of strawberry blonde, a woman would call it. Eyebrows and mustache to match. And his eyes were a very pale blue color. The color of ice when it freezes over Lake Tahoe, if you know what I mean."

"Yes. It does have a rather unusual shade. Your powers of observation are quite good, sir."

The clerk brightened at this comment and added, "I remember something else about the man's eyes—they made me shiver. He never smiled once. Wasn't mean or nasty, but all business. He wore that new style of Stetson—white with a flat brim and high crown."

"Good," Darby said, his mental picture now complete. "How did he announce himself when he arrived at the desk?"

"He said only that he wanted to call on Miss Beavers. I

told him that we could not give him her room number but, if he would take a seat in the lobby, we would deliver his message. After that, it would be up to her if she wanted to receive him or not."

"And he agreed?"

"Yes. He took that easy chair right over there and waited very calmly. He never once took his eyes off the staircase, not for a second, until Miss Beavers made her appearance."

"What was the message that he had delivered?"

The clerk frowned in concentration. "I . . . I don't think I remember."

"Think, man!"

"Ahhh," the clerk gulped, tearing out his handkerchief and mopping the perspiration from his brow. "Let's see. He said . . . yes! 'Tell her to come down if she wants to see . . . Jim . . . Tracy'!"

"Are you sure?"

"Yes! Positive, because I even asked him to repeat the name so there could be no embarrassing mistake."

"Jim Tracy?" Darby's hopes plummeted. He'd never heard the name before, not from Dolly or anyone else. "Have you ever heard of that name?"

"Never. And I'm afraid no one at the Riverfront has ever heard of Mr. Tracy, either. We talked about it for days. It's a complete mystery to all of us who he was or why Miss Beavers left so suddenly with no explanation a few hours later."

"Did Miss Beavers seem upset when she saw this man?"

The clerk reflected for a long moment, then said, " 'Upset' is not the word I'd use. But she did look pale. And you know how cheerful she usually is, Mr. Buckingham, always giggling and having a compliment for everyone. But not when she came down those stairs that day. No, sir! She was as serious as Mr. Tracy. No smile, no nothing. She was like a different woman. I asked her if everything was all right or not."

"And she said?"

"She said she thought everything was going to work out for the best."

"Those were her exact words?"

"Yes." The clerk shrugged. "Those were her *only* words until she checked out a few hours later."

"And without a message for me?"

"I'm afraid not, Mr. Buckingham."

Darby shook his head. He didn't understand this at all. "Did anyone think to ask the sheriff if he ever heard of Jim Tracy?"

"Well . . ."

Darby could see they hadn't. "Then I'll go see him right now. And if he hasn't heard of Mr. Tracy, then I'll go to the newspaper office and everyone else in town until I get to the bottom of this affair."

"Sir, may I offer a suggestion?"

Darby had been about to pivot and leave but now he stopped. "I'm listening."

"Mr. Buckingham, Sheriff Bill Pate was gunned down just three weeks ago. Why don't you get a good night's sleep? If you'll excuse me, sir, you look bushed. Maybe you can pick up a trail tomorrow, but not tonight."

"He's probably right," Austin said. "We could use some sleep. Things might look brighter tomorrow morning."

Darby supposed they made sense. "Very well," he growled, "two adjoining rooms."

"Would you like Miss Beavers's room? Business has been slow and it hasn't been used since the day that she left."

Darby's inclination was to say no, but he changed his mind on the slim chance that some clue might be found. "Very well."

Ten minutes later, Darby was alone in the room, overwhelmed by the lingering scent of Dolly's perfume and the memories of their last night together. He made a quick but thorough search of the room and was not surprised to see that it had been cleaned and any clues that might have been left behind were now gone.

Dolly's presence, however, was still very strong and the nearness of her sent the Derby Man out for a long walk along the dark, cold Truckee River.

"Jim Tracy," he repeated to himself. "Who are you?"

He was so absorbed with his ruminations that he did not see the three big muggers until they blocked his path.

"Your money or a broken head," the tallest man hissed, tapping his palm with a short club of hickory.

The other two tensed. One had a knife and the most powerful of the three just stood ape-like with a blank expression on his flat, brutish face.

Darby raised his fists and a tight smile formed on his lips. "Gentlemen, you won't understand this, but I am in your debt."

The trio exchanged confused glances. "He's looney as hell," the man with the billy finally decided out loud as he advanced. "When I crack open his skull, I'll bet we find that his brains are scrambled eggs."

"If they aren't already, they will be," the man with the knife hissed.

Darby crouched just slightly. His neck sank into his round hump of shoulders and his blood began to surge with anticipation. This attempted mugging, he knew, was just what the doctor ordered.

"Get him," the apish man hollered.

The tall one sprang forward but so did the Derby Man, and his big right fist arced upward with the force of a locomotive's piston. His knuckles caught the tall man in the solar plexus and broke him in half at the waist before lifting him completely off the ground. Darby grabbed his arm and spun him in a full circle before launching him into the ice-cold Truckee River.

Before Darby turned around, the man with the knife attacked and he was as quick as a ferret. Twice, his knife blade glinted in the moonlight but Darby was able to leap away from it, although his coat was sliced to ribbons.

"Give me your wallet, mister! Give it to me now and you can still walk away without spilled guts."

Darby shook his head. He motioned the two men forward. "Come on," he panted.

The knife man sleeved his running nose and looked to the ape man. "Let's get this done, Ernie."

"But what about Tom! He looks to be drowning!"

"To hell with him! Let's take this guy now!"

Darby put his back to a tree. The man with the knife was good and very fast. He was the real danger. Ernie was ox-strong and ox-stupid. All muscle, no brains. Darby knew how to handle muscle.

"I'm going to carve you like a fat Christmas goose, mister!" the knife-wielder said. His eyes flicked to the big man. "Grab and hold him, Ernie!"

Ernie lunged forward, his powerful arms outstretched like a great snare. It was easy to see their battle plan. Ernie would grab Darby and tie him up for an instant while his partner used his knife. It was obvious that they'd done this before. But now, Darby shot a straight left jab that connected with Ernie's jaw like the swinging end of a telegraph pole.

"Owww!" Ernie cried as he staggered forward and managed to fall into Darby. During the instant it took to throw the man aside, Darby felt a pain searing into his side. He'd been stabbed, and had it not been for the notepad he carried, he might have taken a fatal strike.

Before taking a second thrust, Darby blindly slashed down with the edge of his hand and had the satisfaction of hearing a bone snap and seeing the knife fall harmlessly to the ground.

Darby attacked with a savagery and precision gained from his years in the ring. He sent two crushing blows to the man's face, shattering a jawbone and pushing in the right cheekbone. Slamming the man up against the tree,

Darby pounded his face into the bark once and then, instead of killing the fellow, dropped him and stepped away.

Darby scooped up the knife. Ernie was on his knees, eyes round with fear; when Darby took a step in his direction, the man cowered in abject terror. "Don't hit me again!"

"Then you'd better get up and run! You and your friends are out of business."

Darby reached inside his suit coat and was not surprised to feel a warm, slick wetness. He gritted his teeth and gingerly probed the wound. A mere scratch, he decided.

"Who . . . who the hell are you!" Ernie cried.

Before Darby could answer, they both heard a faint cry for help and turned to see the first man bobbing frantically in the swift river.

"Can you swim, Ernie?"

"Uh, yeah, but . . ."

Darby didn't wait to hear the rest. He hauled Ernie to his feet, set him into a fast backpedal and then shoved him into the river.

Ernie wasn't much of a swimmer, but then he wasn't much of a fighter either, despite his great size and strength. Darby turned his back on the lot of them and resumed his solitary walk. The altercation had cleared his mind and raised his spirits because at least fighting was something he could do and it brought all a man's faculties into sharp focus.

Ernie began to cry for help too but the Derby Man didn't notice as he continued his brisk walk in the moonlight.

Who, he asked himself once more, was this Jim Tracy?

THREE

"JIM TRACY? Sorry, Mr. Buckingham, but I've never heard of the man," Deputy Homer Wolf said with a shake of his head.

Darby described the man in detail, then said, "Have you ever seen anyone like that? He sounds like the kind of gent you'd notice in a crowd."

"I'm afraid not," Wolf replied. "You see, with all the traffic funneling back and forth to the Comstock Lode, well sir, hundreds of new faces are passing through Reno every week. Maybe you should go up to Virginia City and talk to Sheriff Elkins. Perhaps he's seen this Jim Tracy fella and Miss Beavers."

"I don't think Tracy is on the Comstock. He bears the stamp of a cattleman."

"There are a few ranches down in the Washoe and the Carson Valleys. Worth a check to see if one is owned by Mr. Tracy. There might even be a deed recorded in Tracy's name filed away at the capitol building in Carson City."

"Good idea." Darby looked to his young friend. Austin shrugged his shoulders. He had no questions.

"Sorry I can't help you," the deputy said. "I knew Miss Dolly real well. Everyone knew and liked her."

"Then how come no one even remembers seeing her leave Reno?" Darby asked with a hint of exasperation. "We've already checked the train station and the Wells

Fargo office. They don't remember seeing her leave with this man."

"Either this Jim Tracy bought a horse for Miss Dolly at one of our local liveries or he brought a couple of his own into Reno. If I were you, I'd try the liveries."

"How many are there?"

"Half dozen, at the most. You'll find them all at either the north or south end of town. And if you don't get the cooperation you're looking for from the proprietors, tell them I said to answer all your questions or I'll see our new fire marshal pays them an inspection visit."

"That ought to do very nicely," Darby said.

Ten minutes later they were standing in the dim, dusty barn of the Ace High Livery explaining the purpose of their call.

"No, sir," the liveryman said, "I'd remember if Miss Dolly was leaving. That woman had a figure that would make a dog drool. I never saw such big—"

"Thanks," Darby said stiffly, turning on his heel and striding away before he lost his temper.

Two hours later, they had covered three liveries and were approaching a fourth. It was a rundown place, strewn with wagons in every stage of disrepair. Four or five pine-pole corrals held some thin horses, a pen of small milk goats and a cow. A collection of mangy dogs snoozed in the shade. Darby saw no one moving around outside so he steered through the debris toward the barn door which listed on a broken strap hinge. On the splitting pine wall over the door were these words scrawled in paint: SID'S LIVERY—I BUY SELL OR TRADE HORSES, GOATS AND MILK COWS.

"What an eyesore!" Austin exclaimed. "I can't imagine anyone with money coming here for horses."

"Maybe not," Darby said, "but I will leave no stone unturned."

"Then let's go."

"Howdee!" chirped a spry little old man with emerald green suspenders and a white beard as he popped out of ned to the Derby Man. "The fella you want left his rse here one morning. He came back that same after-oon with Miss Beavers and traded his saddle mount in for horse and buggy."

Darby's heart leapt. "Do you still have the saddle horse?"

"Damn right. It's as fine an animal as you'd ever want to ride. But your minute's worth of information is long past."

Darby admired the man's fierce spirit. "All right," he said, dragging out a wad of bills. When Sid reached for them, Darby shook his head and put the money back into his pocket. "You'll be well paid—but not until I leave."

"How do I know that?"

"Because," Austin interrupted, "this is the Derby Man. Surely you've heard of him and know—"

"I've heard of him, but that don't mean you're him."

"And it doesn't matter one way or the other right now," Darby snapped. "So just show me Jim Tracy's saddle horse, and I'll pay you five dollars."

The man's jaw was jutting out defiantly but now he relaxed. He'd board a horse an entire week for five dollars. "You promise?"

"I do."

"All right. Come along then."

The leprechaun snapped his green suspenders and led them into his rickety old barn. Shafts of light beamed through the ceiling and walls, enough to reveal piles of broken axles and wheels. If it had been darker, they might have broken their necks navigating through the mess to reach a line of dilapidated box stalls, mostly filled with milk goats and calves. Darby accidentally stepped on a sleeping cat and the thing shrieked and almost gave him heart failure before vanishing into the wagon wreckage.

"That old tomcat will never learn," Sid complained. "You can bet your fanny that, one of these days, a horse is going to stomp him flat."

"You ever think about lighting a match to this place?" Austin said cryptically.

the barn. He sized up Darby and Austi
and grinned, all gums, no teeth. Smoking
he fit Darby's notion of an Irish leprechau
Sid and I own this fine establishment. So wh
you gentlemen today?"

"Just a little information," Darby said, takin
hard, crusty hand in his own bear paw.

"Information?" The man puffed smoke, his g
"Information won't pay my feed bills, mister. I ain
time of day for free information."

"Here," Darby said, handing Sid a dollar. "Now
free."

The leprechaun slipped the dollar into his torn
pocket. "Dollar will buy you a minute."

"That's all I'll need. Have you seen a woman nam
Dolly Beavers and a man named Jim Tracy?" Darb
quickly described the pair.

The little man's eyes narrowed and he rubbed his horny hands together. "What if I have?"

Darby was not in a mood to play games. He reached out and grabbed Sid, hauling him to his toes. "If you have," he growled, "tell me about them right now!"

"Let go of me!" Sid cried. "Who in the hell are you!"

Darby put the man down. "I'm a man who's about out of patience."

"What about money? You run out of that too?"

"I've money for information," Darby said, "but this concerns Miss Beavers's life. It would go very hard if you lied."

Sid poked the stem of his corncob pipe at Darby. "I'm no liar. I'm a man of high principles!"

"Sure you are," Austin drawled.

Sid's eyes flashed and he doubled up his fists and took a step toward Austin. "Why you pretty-faced dandy, I'll . . ."

Darby moved between them. "We're here to find Miss Beavers—not to fight. What can you tell us, Sid?"

Sid fussed and glared at Austin for a moment, then

"It's been suggested once or twice by the town council and the fire marshal who all got nothing better to do than nag anyone trying to make an honest livin'."

Austin muttered something unintelligible which Sid fortunately chose to ignore as he announced, "Here we go! Finest cow pony, or just ridin' horse, in Reno!"

"I can hardly see him," Darby complained as he squinted into the murky darkness. "Can we take him outside for a better look?"

"You interested in buyin' him?"

"Maybe."

"Okay, then stand back."

"Stand back?"

"He's a mite obstreperous, but I'll wager he's faster than a fox in a hen house."

"I'm sure," Darby said, bumping into Austin as they retreated back through the maze toward the door.

A few minutes later, the liveryman emerged, struggling to control a big palomino gelding whose eyes rolled around like marbles in an empty fruit jar. "Easy, easy, damn you!"

Darby knew that he could not have handled the horse himself, but Austin moved right up to the palomino and grabbed ahold of its halter. "Easy, boy," he soothed, reaching up to scratch the gelding behind its ear. To Darby's amazement, and to the liveryman's obvious astonishment, the palomino settled right down.

"Well now, would you lookee there!" the liveryman exclaimed, handing Austin the lead rope and retreating to a safe distance. "The dandy ain't got no respect for his elders, but he can sure make horse-talk."

"We had a stable full of them while I was growing up," Austin explained. "They were my sanity. I speak and they'll usually listen."

"I can see that," Darby said, moving in a wide circle around the magnificent beast until he saw the brand on its left hindquarters. "What brand is that?" he asked Sid.

"Rocking T."

"The T is for Tracy, I'll wager," Darby said. "Do you know where that ranch is to be found?"

Sid shook his head. "Nope. But it's not a Nevada brand. If it was, I'd have seen it a time or two over the last twenty years I've owned this fine establishment."

"Blast," Darby muttered. "Is there anyone who might know where it is?"

"If I were you, I'd ask the cowboys. Most of them are drifters anyway. They'll mostly shag in from Arizona, Wyoming, Montana and even Colorado. You ask around, one of 'em is bound to know where the Rocking T Ranch is located. But it's not in this state."

"Thanks," Darby said, trying to hide his disappointment by telling himself that he had at least found some clue to Dolly's whereabouts.

"Your thanks," Sid said pointedly, "won't come close to paying my feed bills."

Darby fished out his money and peeled off five dollars. "This ought to help."

The man grinned. "Mr. Derby Man, if you ever need a good horse, you come by and I'll do you right."

"I'll keep that in mind," Darby promised. "One last question. Do you have any idea where Jim Tracy and Miss Beavers were heading? Perhaps he said something that would give me a clue as to their destination."

"Afraid not. I can tell you for certain that they rode east toward Fallon. I watched him and the lady until they rounded the corner."

Austin handed the lead rope back to Sid. "Did Miss Beavers say anything?"

Sid licked his lips. "Didn't have to say a word, and if she had, I don't think I'd remember. You could say her physical charms sort of muddied my attention."

"I see."

Sid patted the gelding. "Young fella, you'd sure look fine astride this flashy palomino. It appears to me like you and this animal get along like old pards. I could give you a hell of a price."

"I'll bet."

"The fella hated to leave him, but the horse won't pull a buggy. Tracy boasted that this horse was good with cattle and he'll do to shoot a rifle off. Said he'd pack moose, elk or white-tailed antelope."

Darby had been about to walk away but now he froze in his tracks. "Jim Tracy said that?"

"He sure did! And I have no reason not to believe the man, 'cause he said it after we'd made our deal. He had nothin' to gain at that point by lyin' to me." Sid looked hopefully at Austin. "You needin' a huntin' pony, young fella?"

"Maybe," Austin said, studying Darby and knowing they were both having the same thoughts.

Darby looked the old man right in the eye. "Sid, where is the best place to hunt white-tailed antelope, moose or elk?"

"In Nevada?" Sid queried.

"No, outside the state."

"Well, mostly to the north in Montana or Wyoming. But you wouldn't have to go that far. Now, you'll still find four-point bucks in these mountains clear down south into California."

"Thanks," Darby said, turning on his heel and marching back toward town.

"What are we going to do now?" Austin asked as he hurried after Darby.

"I'm going to introduce you to the Western saloon. Most people in this town know me and, if you're at my side, you won't be bothered because of your dress."

"I don't need your protection! I can take care of myself."

"I'm sure you can," Darby said. "But some of the cowboys can be a bit rough when they think they've cornered a real dude. If I'm along, things might go a little more smoothly."

Austin wasn't pleased but he was smart enough not to

make an issue of the matter. And Darby's mind was too preoccupied to pay attention to his objections anyway.

Darby had spent enough time in Reno to know which saloons catered to cowboys, which to miners and which to merchants, businessmen and tradesmen. Now, he stopped before the entrance to the Buckaroo Bar. The door was wide open and he could see that the place was packed with rough cowboys. The talk and the laughter were loud and coarse.

"You'd better stick close," Darby warned.

Austin peeked inside. All he could see were Stetsons and booted men wearing six-guns on their hips. "You ever been in this one before?" he asked, trying not to betray his sudden nervousness.

"Nope. But it's a free country and if we want to find out about the Rocking T, I can't imagine a better place."

Darby started to enter but Austin grabbed his coatsleeve. "Wait just a minute."

"What is it?"

"Well," Austin stammered, "I—I was just wondering how you intended to do this. I mean . . . are we supposed to buy drinks for everyone and make an announcement or . . ."

"That's a fine idea!" Darby said, jamming an unlit Cuban cigar between his teeth.

"Well, okay then," Austin said, screwing his derby down tight. "That's just what we'll do."

Darby suppressed a grin. Austin had mentioned something about having studied the "scientific" method of fisticuffs. He might even have been in his collegiate boxing club. But that kind of fighting and the kind he was likely to encounter inside the Buckaroo Bar were entirely different. And while scientific methods were important in many fields, the only science that mattered in a barroom brawl was the ability to stay erect and keep punching.

"Just let me do all the talking," Darby said with confidence. "Cowboys do like to fight and they can be pretty clannish, but they'll warm up real fast with a few free drinks. They're not about to bite the hand that feeds them."

"Whatever you say, Mr. Buckingham."

Darby pushed into the doorway, filling it completely. The room was smokey, and somewhere in the back, beyond the crowd, he could hear an out-of-tune piano and a couple of cowboys singing a bawdy version of "The Old Chisholm Trail."

Their entrance stopped conversation at the near end of the bar, and when a sweaty, overworked bartender glanced up at them, his professional smile died. He said something to a couple of hard-looking riders, then laid his bar rag down and left his station to come and intercept Darby and Austin.

"Gentlemen," he said, "I'm guessing you probably just arrived from Boston or someplace nice, but you must understand that this is a *Buckaroo* bar. Gentlemen dressed like you need to stroll about two blocks up the street to the Continental Club where I promise you'll be much happier."

"This looks fine to me," Darby said cheerfully. "Doesn't it to you, Mr. Applegate?"

Austin managed to nod his head in agreement but his eyes were fixed on the line of cowboys now glaring in their direction.

The bartender scowled. "Gentlemen," he said, "I don't want to seem inhospitable, but I'm afraid I'm going to have to ask you to remove yourselves. It ain't . . . well . . . it ain't healthy for gentlemen like yourselves in my establishment."

Darby's cigar wagged back and forth, once, twice. He raised his hand and bellowed, "Drinks for everyone!"

His cry stilled the room for an instant and then brought a loud chorus of cheers. Men began to chug down their beers, slamming empty glasses onto the bar and calling for the much more expensive whiskey.

"Well, gentlemen, step right in and belly up to my bar!" the proprietor hollered, rushing back to his station and grabbing a pair of full whiskey bottles.

Darby pushed his way right up to the bar and took the space of two ordinary men. Austin managed to wedge himself in beside Darby while the bartender walked up and down, literally splashing whiskey over a solid line of empty glasses. By the time he returned to Darby, he had emptied the two bottles.

"That'll be ten dollars, sir!"

Darby slapped a hundred dollars down on the polished bar. "Keep them filled!"

"That's the stuff!" the bartender cried, snatching up the money and shouting, "Three more rounds on Mr. . . ."

All heads swung to Darby and Austin. "On who, sir?" the bartender asked.

"The Derby Man!" a cowboy shouted. "That there is Mr. Darby Buckingham, the famous dime novelist!"

A cheer went up around the room and everyone hoisted his glass in a toast to Darby.

By the time Darby's money was spent, he and Austin were the most popular two men in Reno. Word of the Derby Man's largess had traveled up and down Virginia Street and every cowboy in town had jammed into the Buckaroo Bar in the hope of getting free drinks.

"Help me up on the bartop," Darby said, feeling his head begin to buzz, "while I can still make a coherent announcement."

"Give me your foot," Austin said, lacing his fingers together in preparation for hoisting Darby.

"Let *me* help him," a huge cowboy said, pushing Austin out of the way and bending over to receive Darby's polished shoe.

"Most kind of you," Darby said, placing his foot into the man's cupped hands.

"Ready?" the huge cowboy asked, winking at his friend.

"Sure."

Austin started to warn Darby, but it was too late. The huge cowboy catapaulted the Derby Man completely over the bartop into the backbar. Darby crashed to the floor under a shower of liquor and glass. He landed on his head and his lights went out.

Austin pivoted to confront the huge cowboy. "You think that was funny?"

The man was laughing so hard that tears were running down his cheeks. Austin filled the cowboy's big mouth with his knuckles. He felt intense pain as the man's teeth lacerated his hand but there was also the wild satisfaction of feeling teeth break—or maybe it was the bones of his own hand; he could not be certain. The cowboy staggered but his friends caught him.

"Get that dandy, Luke! Beat his face in!"

Luke shook away the cobwebs. He spat blood and teeth and then cursed as he swung a massive fist at Austin.

Austin ducked. Instinctively, he banged two lightning-fast body punches into the huge cowboy's gut. To his surprise and dismay, the cowboy threw back his head and gave a deep belly-laugh. "You better say your prayers, kid!"

"Uh-oh," Austin breathed an instant before the man grabbed him by the front of his coat, pinned him against the bar and nearly took his head off with two thunderous overhand rights.

Austin's vision swam. He staggered forward, grabbed Luke and clung to the much more powerful man, trying to clear his senses.

Luke easily threw him off. Dimly, Austin saw the man grin and wipe a smear of blood on his sleeve. Luke took a slug of whiskey, nice and slow, then doubled up his fist and prepared to finish what he'd started.

Austin would have ducked but a cowboy held him erect and Austin heard the man shout, "Just make sure it's this pilgrim's face you rearrange and not mine by mistake, Luke!"

If there was a reply, Austin didn't hear it. He twisted free, ducked a looping overhand and managed to bang Luke in the nose, but it didn't break. Hell, it didn't even bleed!

"You had enough?" Austin shouted.

The room exploded with hoots and laughter. Luke was the only man in the bar who didn't appreciate the joke. "Come on, you scrawny little fop!"

Austin risked a quick glance over the bar, praying that Darby would revive to save him from being bludgeoned to death by this angry giant. But the Derby Man was on his hands and knees, trying to clear away his own cobwebs.

Luke chuckled. "You're just a little yellow pissant, ain't you!"

Austin grabbed a shot glass of whiskey and downed it in a gulp. "Come on!" he cried, his voice nearly breaking. "Come and eat some more teeth!"

It was a completely ridiculous challenge, comical to the cowboys, many of whom burst out laughing. But Austin knew that if he hadn't issued the challenge, he'd have lost his nerve completely and bolted out the door, leaving the Derby Man to fend for himself.

"Give him room," a cowboy shouted and a small circle formed around Austin and Luke.

"Hell," another cowboy laughed, "he don't need but enough room to fall."

Austin could feel the cowboys pushing at him and he waited on shaky legs while Luke took another drink, then set his glass down very deliberately and raised his big fists.

Hit him first! Austin thought. Hit him as hard and as fast as you can. It's your only chance!

Austin lunged forward, his fist a blur until it struck Luke in the eye and knocked him back a step.

A cheer for the underdog went up but Austin didn't have time to enjoy it. His hands were flashing, peppering Luke's face, drawing blood and curses. Luke roared in pain and came windmilling forward. Austin ducked and dove at the man's knees. It wasn't the way he'd been taught to fight, but it was the only way he could see to avoid a roundhouse punch that would knock him senseless.

Luke toppled and tried to grab Austin as he fell, but the Easterner wiggled loose and was on his feet first.

"Kick him!" a man shouted. "Goddammit, kid, it's your only hope!"

Austin drew back his foot and he could have kicked Luke right in his bloodied face but he didn't have the heart. Instead, he waited until the huge cowboy clambered to his feet and then he hit him twice more before Luke got a shoulder into his chest and drove him into the bar, rattling glasses.

Austin struggled to free himself but Luke wasn't about to let him go. Again, the cowboy grabbed his coat with his left hand, then smashed brutal overhand rights to Austin's face until his legs buckled.

A gun exploded close by. Luke froze and turned. Austin tried to focus but he was seeing double and his mouth was full of blood. Luke dropped him and Austin hit the floor, wanting to lose consciousness and drown in his red sea of pain. "Enough!" Darby's command cut through the fog and Austin saw his idol charge around the end of the bar as the dime novelist shoved his smoking derringer into his coat pocket.

Not another word was spoken by either Darby or Luke as they attacked each other. The shouts and rooting cries that had filled the Buckaroo Bar a moment earlier died. Everyone held his breath, got the hell out of the way and let the two big men wage war.

Austin heard labored grunts punctuated by the staccato *thud* of fists exploding against flesh. Shoe leather scraped floorboards and legs bent, quivering, as fists ripped and pounded. At first Darby was driven back a few steps, then Luke. Then they stood toe to toe, bashing each other until Luke howled and Darby drove the cowboy back one step, then another, and sent him into a reeling retreat toward the front door.

Darby was terrible to behold with his fighting blood aroused. The last of Darby's punches sent the huge cowboy flying into the street. Darby went after him and Austin was almost trampled to death in the stampede as men tried to get outside to see the worst beating they'd ever witnessed.

Austin wobbled to his feet. "He's going to kill him!" he cried as he staggered toward the door. The fight was over. Darby, surrounded by a crowd, was lighting a cigar and talking to the men around him, asking them if any had heard of the Rocking T Ranch.

Austin shook his head and touched his battered face. He was covered with blood, mostly his own but maybe some of Luke's, too. He heard a cowboy say something about Wyoming and he heard newfound excitement in Darby's questioning voice.

Austin swiveled around and managed to reach the bar, where he clung, his chest heaving. His hand snaked out and he found an uncorked bottle of whiskey. He drank, feeling the fire wash away the shame of being beaten so easily. He remembered his hollow bragging about being able to handle himself in a frontier fight, and now it mocked him.

"Mr. Applegate," Darby said, pushing back into the bar with a crowd of cowboys in his wake, "would you pour me a glass, too?"

Austin cocked his head sideways and could not imagine —no matter how awful he looked—that he was any worse than the Derby Man. "Do I look as bad as you?"

"Worse," Darby said, raising his glass in a rock-steady fist. "But by the time we reach Wyoming, we'll look as good as new."

"Is that where we're going?"

Darby drank, then refilled his glass, puffing steadily on his cigar.

"It is."

"When?"

"If you are well enough to ride, we'll leave tomorrow morning."

"It isn't my *butt* that just took a beating. Don't worry, I can still ride."

Darby tossed down another whiskey, then slipped his powerful arm around Austin and helped him toward the door as the cowboys cheered and tried to pound him on the back in congratulation.

"A bath, fresh clothes and a big steak dinner," the Derby Man was saying as they weaved down the street, "and we'll be like a pair of new men."

Austin didn't believe that for a single minute, but he knew that there was nothing in the world that would keep him from accompanying the Derby Man tomorrow morning when he left for Wyoming.

FOUR

WHEN Darby and Austin arrived at Sid's Livery the next morning after breakfast, the old man was just finishing feeding his menagerie of barnyard livestock. A pair of billy goats jumped up onto the skeleton of an old Conestoga wagon and bleated a greeting.

Sid turned around and his eyes bugged. "Holy smokes! What happened to you fellas?"

Darby was in good spirits and quite optimistic despite being sore and having his left eye swollen almost shut. Now that he felt sure that he would find Jim Tracy and then Dolly, he was feeling hopeful.

"Sid," he said, "we're leaving for Wyoming on the train this afternoon. There's a stock car in which we can rent space for a couple of good horses."

Sid grinned. "Why, there sure is!"

"Of course," Darby added quickly, "I can buy good mounts in Wyoming when we arrive. After all, there is certainly no shortage of *cheap* horseflesh in that cowboy country."

Sid's grin slipped. "I suppose not."

"However," Austin added, "I sort of took a liking to that palomino. If the price is right, we might buy our horses from you and then we'd know that we had good stock."

Sid showed his gums. "Why, now, you fellas are real

smart to look at it thataway! And, Mr. Buckingham, I have just the horse for you!"

"I don't like horses," Darby said, "but I've come to accept the fact that they're a necessary evil in the West. Let's see the beast."

The "beast," as Darby called it, was all alone, penned in an enclosure stout enough to contain a herd of rhino, a creature to which this horse bore a certain structural resemblance. One glance told Darby that the animal was fit only for an ore wagon or a plow. It was huge, seventeen hands tall, two axe-handles wide and attached to feet as big around as barrel hoops. The beast was also extraordinarily ugly and mean-looking.

Darby stared at the horse, which caused it to flatten its mulish ears.

"Sid, you can't be serious! I'd have to have a ladder just to get on and off him. And look at the way he lays his ears back at the mere sight of me."

"Just shows he's interested in you, Mr. Buckingham."

"Well, I don't share that interest. He's not only a brute, but he's much too big and tall."

"I suppose so," Sid allowed, looking at Darby's short, powerful legs. "Anyway, I've got another horse that you'll like a whole lot better."

Darby remained silent but jumped when the huge abomination snapped its yellow teeth at him as they edged around the massively reinforced corral.

"Now, this one," Sid said, pointing to a pen where a handsome sorrel gelding with four white stockings and a blaze on its decidedly intelligent face was grazing placidly, "is my favorite. His name is Hallelujah and I bought him from a little old preacher who just used him on his ministry circuit. Treated him like a little dog, he did. Fed him right out of his hand and never run or abused him. He's gentle as a kitten, sound as a dollar and as good-hearted as Jesus Christ himself."

"What happened to the preacher?" Austin asked.

Sid clucked his tongue and shook his head in regret. "Mr. Applegate, that poor preacher got a little rheumatism in his back and had to trade this fine animal for a little buggy mare. But if that God-fearin' man were here right now, he'd swear to you that he loved Hallelujah like his only son."

Darby stifled a groan. "How much are you asking for this only son of a preacher man?"

"A hundred dollars." Sid winked. "But only because you're a friend."

"If it gets any deeper . . . ," Austin said, leaving the sentence unfinished.

Darby frowned. "How much for the palomino Jim Tracy left behind?"

"Another hundred dollars. You're stealing him at that price."

Darby knew the man's asking price was outrageous. "I'll pay one hundred dollars for the both of them and you throw in the tack."

"What!"

Darby looked at Austin. "Good saddle horses are real cheap up in Wyoming because they're thicker than fleas. Besides, we won't have to rent that stock car."

"Right," Austin said, turning with the Derby Man to leave.

"Now, wait a minute!" Sid cried, charging after them with the goats in tow. "I didn't say that I wouldn't deal a little. But a hundred dollars for two of the best horses in the state of Nevada and all the tack—you're trying to fleece me!"

"All right. My final offer is a hundred twenty-five. But only *if* Mr. Applegate and I consider the tack to be in first-rate condition. Take it or leave it."

Sid's lips turned down at the corners. "I'll take it."

"Good. Let's see your best saddles."

Sid was so unhappy he kicked out at one of the goats but missed. "I'll throw these two goats in for nothin'," he crabbed, "if you promise not to let them out of that stock car until you reach Wyoming."

"No, thanks."

"They barbecue up real nice."

"Not interested," Darby said.

Sid didn't stop cussing all the way back to his barn.

Darby soon left Austin to oversee the inspection of their new tack. Before leaving, he gave orders that both horses were to be shod immediately and extended Austin enough money to pay for everything.

"I insist on paying my own way," the young man said, ignoring the money. "I won't be a financial burden to you, Mr. Buckingham."

"Very well," Darby said, pocketing the money because he knew that young Applegate could well afford to pay his share of expenses. "You take care of this horse business to your satisfaction and I'll buy whatever I think we might need for the train trip back to Wyoming."

"It's a shame that we had to come all the way back from Promontory Point only to retrace our steps."

"Life works like that sometimes," Darby said, walking off.

"Oh, Mr. Buckingham!" Austin called.

Darby stopped. "Yes?"

Austin gave him fifty dollars. "I'd like you to buy me a double-barreled shotgun just like the one you own."

"Might be better if you had a Winchester," Darby said. "That way, we'd be covered both short and long range. I'd use a rifle if I could hit anything."

Austin thought it over a moment and then he nodded and handed Darby another fifty dollars. "Very well, then, a Winchester repeater and maybe a six-gun, for the same reasons you just gave me."

"Good! And once we reach Wyoming, perhaps I could give you a few pointers on how to fight Western-style."

Austin grinned lopsidedly because one side of his face was all puffy. "I take it that means you weren't impressed."

"On the contrary," Darby said, "I was *very* impressed with your courage. I'd just like to see you win the next fight."

Austin shook his head. "I doubt I'll ever be able to beat a man the size and strength of Luke."

"Nonsense," Darby said. "You just have to be a little more selective in where you target your punches."

"Sir?"

Darby plucked a Cuban from his jacket pocket and bit off the tip. He lit it and inhaled, then exhaled with a sigh. "Next time," he said, "punch a man like that in the throat."

"What!"

"You heard me," Darby said. "If he can't breathe, he can't very well fight. Now, let me see your hands."

Austin stuck them out and Darby inspected them carefully. "You're tall, very fast and athletic, Mr. Applegate, but you're not a big-boned man and you'll break these hands against the skull of someone like Luke. You must learn to strike the *soft* body parts to compensate for your own physical limitations."

"Like the throat and . . . where else?"

"You're a writer, aren't you?" Darby said with a wink. "Use your God-given imagination."

The Rocking T Ranch, Darby had learned, was situated to the north of a little Union Pacific Railroad stop named Whiskey Creek. It was a thousand miles away but there was now a transcontinental railroad to carry them and Darby's spirits were high. The trip itself went without incident, and when the conductor announced that the next stop was Whiskey Creek, Darby and Austin were more than eager to disembark.

"Good luck to you, gentlemen," the conductor said as Austin and Darby climbed down from the train to face a cold, hard wind that came ripping off the distant Laramie Mountains. "You're sure enough going to need it here."

"What is that supposed to mean!" Austin shouted into the wind.

Darby thought the answer self-evident. While helping the Union Pacific lay track west toward Promontory Point, he'd seen Whiskey Creek spring up like all the other little overnight rail towns; one day booming, then two weeks later packed up and leapfrogging westward so that they could continue relieving the mostly Irish construction workers of their hard-earned wages.

"Look around you, Mr. Applegate, and I think you'll see what the conductor meant."

Austin used both hands to pull his derby down until his ears were bent and the hat could not take flight. He surveyed the single row of mostly boarded-up stores. There were more tumbleweeds moving down the street than men, wagons or horses.

"Maybe we should have got off at Laramie," Austin said, glancing back at the train. "Or gone on over the mountains to Cheyenne. Maybe we *still* should, Mr. Buckingham."

"Not much point in that. We'd only have to ride back this way again. Come on. Let's make sure that they don't cripple our horses during the unloading and that no one steals our tack."

Austin picked up his luggage and the two men trudged along the railroad bed feeling the sting of wind-driven cinders.

Their horses were quickly saddled, bridled and unloaded, and within minutes the train's locomotive blew its steam whistle and jolted into motion. Darby tied his valises to his saddle and studied Whiskey Creek with a critical eye. He judged that there might be two hundred permanent residents here surviving off railroad jobs or catering to the ranching community. And, most likely, Jim Tracy was one of their main customers. They'd know the man, perhaps even know about Miss Beavers.

"Looks like a livery over there!" Austin shouted into the cold wind. "Might be the only one in town."

"Not much doubt about that," Darby said, striking off with his head down and leading his cold, gaunt and miserable gelding.

The livery had a pretty fair barn; unlike Sid's establishment, it was very clean and well ordered. In every stall, the horses were well fed and brushed sleek.

"How long are you going to be staying?" the liveryman asked as he forked good grass hay to their horses.

"Not long, we hope," Austin said. "Does the wind always blow this cold and hard?"

The man put his pitchfork down and shook his head. He was hollow-cheeked and looked tired and unwell. Hooking a thumb into a pair of ragged bib overalls, he considered Austin's question for almost a minute. Watching him, Darby thought this cold, constant wind and the hard life of a dying railroad town had probably aged and even addled the poor fellow. The man's shoes were worn out and he looked as if he hadn't eaten a square meal in a month.

"Well, sir," the man finally drawled, "it just blows hard and cold ten months of the year—the other two, you bake."

"Is there a decent hotel in this town?"

"Tent or board?"

"Board."

"That'll be the Medicine Lodge Hotel. Only two-storied place they didn't haul over to Rawlins when the construction crews passed through these mountains. One good thing, you won't have to worry about that hotel being filled."

He giggled and Darby looked away, somehow a little disturbed by the man and his grim circumstances. When he saw people like this, living so poor that each day was a battle to eke out a livelihood, he was reminded of his own good fortune.

"Here," Darby said, giving the man an extra dollar. "We'll want them grained heavy and brushed. I expect to be leaving in the morning."

"You might like to stay. Whiskey Creek doesn't look like much now, but it's a real friendly town with nice folks." The man winked. "We got a gal named Ginger that works at the Medicine Lodge. She's no spring chicken anymore, but she'll warm you up in a hurry for two dollars."

"We'll keep that in mind," Darby said stiffly. "In the meantime, can you tell us how to find the Rocking T Ranch?"

"Why sure! It's about thirty miles north on Lodgepole Creek."

"Big ranch?"

"Ain't none bigger in this part of Wyoming," the liveryman said. "Probably takes in ten thousand acres, not counting the mountain pasture where they run sheep and cattle in the summertime."

"Does Mr. Tracy ever visit Whiskey Creek?" Darby asked.

"Who's Mr. Tracy?"

"Why, the man who owns the Rocking T Ranch."

"That'd be Mr. Jim Talbot. Never heard of no Mr. Tracy."

"Are you sure?" Darby asked in confusion.

"Course, I'm sure! The Talbots have always owned that ranch. Old James Talbot homesteaded most of it over twenty years ago. Now, his son Jim operates the spread."

Darby glanced at Austin who shrugged, obviously surprised and confused. The Derby Man looked back at the liveryman. "Just so I am sure that I understand, is this Jim Talbot a tall fella with pale red hair, a sunburned face and who wears a big turquoise ring set in gold?"

"That's Mr. Talbot, all right." The man frowned. "Why so many questions?"

"How often," Austin interrupted, "does Mr. Talbot visit Whiskey Creek?"

"Hard to say. He owns part of it but, more and more, he and his boys trade in Cheyenne. Sure does hurt the town."

"Do you know anything about a woman that he brought in from Nevada? She has blonde hair and blue eyes."

"You'd be askin' about Mrs. Talbot. Yeah, I seen her again. Pretty as ever."

Darby gulped. "You called her Mrs. Talbot?"

"Well, of course! But she left Mr. Talbot years ago, takin' all of us by surprise, and we never seen her since. Now, her showing up like this—well, sir—it did set tongues to waggin'."

Darby suddenly wanted a stiff drink. "Thanks," he managed to say as he headed for the door.

Austin was right by his side, and as they bulled outside into the hard wind, he shouted, "It doesn't necessarily mean the way it sounds."

"Doesn't it?" Darby did not stop walking.

"There must be *some* explanation."

"Don't worry," Darby yelled into the wind, "we'll hear it before we leave Wyoming. And we'll hear it from none other than Miss Beavers herself!"

Austin nodded. This town, this wind and this news all conspired to fill him with a sense of impending doom. He could see that Darby Buckingham was terribly upset. And who could blame the poor man? After all, it was obvious that he'd known nothing about Dolly being married. And what of this confusion between the names Tracy and Talbot?

None of it made any sense to Austin. Later tonight, he'd sit down and put all of his confusing thoughts down on paper. Maybe then he could see some logic, some sense in this mysterious puzzle. One thing was sure, if Dolly was still married and had decided to return to this Talbot or Tracy fellow voluntarily, it was going to be a devastating blow to Mr. Buckingham. It was clear that he loved Miss Beavers very much.

Well, Austin thought, if the Derby Man's heart gets broken, I'll just do what I can to comfort him until the misery passes.

Austin had had the pleasure of knowing many women. A few of them he'd loved and one girl named Annie Rooney had broken his heart like a cheap goblet and then ground it under her pretty heel. So he understood the pain of real heartache, understood it all too well.

In the morning, Darby was somber and exhibited no appetite when a cheerful waiter took the breakfast orders in their hotel dining room. Austin could see lines of weariness under his eyes and he knew the Derby Man had spent a sleepless and troubled night.

Darby looked up at his young friend. "Last night I went out for a walk. No mugging, though I'd have welcomed it as a distraction."

The Derby Man shook his head in bewilderment. "Isn't it something how a man thinks he knows *everything* about a woman only to discover that he knows practically nothing. Miss Beavers . . . or rather Mrs. Talbot . . . ," he corrected bitterly, "was a complete stranger."

"I don't believe that," Austin said.

"How could you *not* believe it!" Then Darby lowered his angry voice. "I'm sorry. I'm just upset and I feel betrayed. I was going to *marry* that woman."

Darby reached for a cigar, then seemed to lose interest. "I've been thinking that it would be better if we just waited for the westbound train and returned to Reno."

"What!"

"I mean it," Darby said quietly. "What's the point in riding thirty miles of mountain trails to visit the Rocking T Ranch? Obviously, Dolly could not be honest with me. To confront her now would only cause us both more pain and humiliation."

"But if you don't talk to her, you'll always wonder why."

"I *know* why," Darby snapped. "She ran away because she was still legally married."

Austin wanted to object but he had no grounds for argument. Maybe Darby Buckingham was right. Why compound the man's heartache?

"The westbound Union Pacific will come back through here in three days," Darby said, studying his hands. "I'm going to be on it. If you want to come along, we can find some other story. Hopefully, one with a happier ending."

"I didn't come out to meet and join you just for happy endings, sir. I came to find adventure."

"This is no adventure," Darby said. "Besides, no reader would enjoy this sad tale of deceit." Darby climbed to his feet. "I think I'll go back upstairs to my room and rest. I slept badly last night and feel a little unwell."

"Of course."

Darby turned and left the room. It seemed to Austin that the man had grown old in a single night.

FIVE

AUSTIN WALKED the entire length of the town of Whiskey Creek in less than three minutes. There just wasn't much to see. A general store, the livery, two saloons, one cafe and a combination saddlemaker and gunsmith shop about covered the list of establishments still operating. Scattered among them were almost a dozen boarded-up businesses, some with their signs missing but others with them painted right on the front. Beeman's Feed, the Whiskey Creek Gazette, Haney's Groceries, Yo Foo's Laundry and a few more empty cafes and saloons. There were plenty of gaps in the business section of the main street, and Austin figured that either entire wooden structures had been dismantled and hauled away or else tents had served as businesses during Whiskey Creek's heyday and had been quickly folded up and carted off to the next rail town.

Austin, restless and troubled, went into the combination saddle and gun shop where a man was seated at a bench working on an old cap-and-ball Navy Colt. They hadn't had the chance to buy a Colt revolver in Reno; maybe this would be as good a time as any.

"Hello," he said to the proprietor.

The gunsmith, a short, stocky man with blue eyes and silver hair, glanced up from the six-gun, measured Austin, then looked back down without so much as a smile of greeting.

Austin cast his eyes about. There were a few old black powder pistols in the gun case along with a couple of Winchesters and a fine Sharps buffalo rifle, but nothing that Austin wanted to buy.

"I would like to purchase a new Colt revolver that's been converted from percussion to cartridge. I don't see any in this case. Do you have any for sale?"

"Nope."

"Can you get any?"

"Nope. Everyone wants 'em converted right now."

"I'd be willing to pay top dollar."

"Not interested."

Austin became annoyed. "Aren't you even interested in making a hefty profit?"

The gunsmith looked up. He was wearing a pair of thin leather gloves with all the fingertips cut out of them and a matching leather vest. "I don't want any profit from the likes of you, mister."

"What's wrong with me?"

"Don't like your damned face."

"Well," Austin huffed, "I don't like yours either!"

He slammed out of the shop, wondering what in the hell kind of businessmen lived in Whiskey Creek. Furious at being treated so meanly, Austin jammed a cigar into his mouth, realized he hadn't cut off the tip, took it out and bit, then spit. He put a match to the cigar and puffed with agitation. He spotted an old man sitting in front of a saloon with his heels resting on the porch rail and his fingers hooked in the ruff of a dog's coat. He looked like a man who'd been in this part of Wyoming for a good long time and who might provide some useful information on the Talbots and their Rocking T Ranch.

Austin marched over and said, "Howdy."

The old man thumbed a shapeless hat up from his eyes and squinted at Austin. The dog banged its tail against the porch twice, then went back to sleep. Austin decided that friendly greetings were not a big thing in Whiskey Creek. He took a chair beside the old fellow. "Mind if I visit?"

"I guess not," the old man said, eying Austin's still bruised face. "Who the hell beat you to a welt?"

"A fella named Luke."

The old man shook his head. "I don't believe I know any Lukes. Did once. But he died of cholera about six years ago. Luke who?"

"I don't know his last name."

"Humph," the old man grunted, spitting a long stream of chewing tobacco into the dusty street. "Well, I hope you stay away from him in the future."

"I will," Austin said. "Have you lived in these parts long?"

"Yep. Came here way before the damned railroad ruined the place."

"I suppose you know Mr. Jim Talbot pretty well, huh?"

"Sure! Hell, everyone knows him. Knew his father, James. He was even meaner than Jim. Gobbled up all the land on the Laramie River. Shot a couple of men back in the summer of '49. Got shot himself and it served the bastard right."

"Has his son shot anyone?"

"Hell, yes!" The old man whipped his head around and squinted at Austin with one cloudy eye, revealing that he was nearly blind. He had bushy white eyebrows, a tobacco-stained mustache and beard, and batwing ears flattened on top by years of wearing a cowboy hat pushed down hard. His hat was a Stetson of some vintage with a snakeskin band and an eagle feather. His hands were very large and the joints were red and swollen. He was as slender as a tule reed and before the years and injuries had whittled him down, he'd once been quite tall.

"But listen here, young man, you don't go tellin' anybody old Bert said that. If it ever got back to Jim, he'd kill me, too!"

"I won't," Austin promised. "I guess men like the Talbots pretty much take what they want."

"They always have." Bert chewed his tobacco thoughtfully. "I used to work for Mr. Talbot. Rode broncs for him nigh onto ten years. He bought the worst outlaws he could find."

"But he never bought one you couldn't ride, did he, old-timer?"

Bert paused for a moment, then said, "I'm bound to say that, a couple times, he did."

"What happened then?"

"Me and some other cowboy would rope, saddle, then drag 'em down to the river. Lead 'em into shallow water where I'd jump off my broke horse onto the outlaw and buck 'im out. Ain't a horse alive that can buck worth a damn in knee-deep water."

Austin made a mental note to use this cowboy knowledge in some future dime novel. It seemed grossly unfair to the horse and not very glamorous, yet entirely sensible from the cowboy's point of view.

"I suppose that's the way to do it."

"Is if you want to keep your job. Mr. Talbot sure admired them outlaws. But he always wanted me to break them hard. He'd make me use a quirt, spurs and a Spanish bit that'd tear their jaws off. He didn't give a damn. Fact is, he liked to watch me whip 'em down to a nubbin."

Austin was shocked. Back east, horses weren't always treated well, but they were too valuable to kill or maim in training. "So why'd you leave Mr. Talbot and the Rocking T Ranch?"

"As I got older and more crippled up every year, more'n more broncs started to buck me off. One stomped the hell out of me the last month I was on the Rocking T's payroll. After that, I couldn't ride the outlaws anymore so the old man hired a new bronc fighter. Told me I could either dig wells or get the hell off his ranch. I left, of course."

"Of course."

The old man spat again. He raked his bent, arthritic fingers through his dog's coat and chewed his tobacco in silence.

"Bert, did you know Mrs. Dolly Talbot?"

"Sure! Before she married, she was Miss Dolly Beavers."

"What can you tell me about her?"

"I could tell you a hell of a lot, but I won't."

Austin's head snapped back. "Why not!"

"Good way to get myself shot, that's why." The old man spat tobacco. "Mr. Talbot is a hard man and he don't like people gossiping about him and his wife. There's a lot of bad feelings between 'em and some dirty laundry, too. But I won't speak of it. No, sir!"

"I'm not asking you to tell me anything that isn't commonly known in Whiskey Creek."

Bert raised his finger and shook it in Austin's face. "Young fella, let me give you a piece of good advice. If it gets back to Mr. Talbot that you're here askin' a lot of questions about him and Dolly, you'll wind up in a pine box."

Austin sighed. "I see." He slipped a ten-dollar bill between Bert's fingers.

"You can keep your dollar, young fella."

"No. You keep it. Maybe you'll tell me who might be willin' to talk about Dolly's past."

"Only a fool."

"All right. Are there any fools in this town?"

Bert was silent for a moment; then he said, "Talk to Ginger."

"The woman who works at the hotel?"

"That's the one. She and Dolly were best friends. They grew up playin' together. Ginger is about the only one in Whiskey Creek that don't give a damn what she says about anybody."

"Thanks," Austin said, coming to his feet. "And by the way, don't let someone cheat you—that's a *ten*-dollar bill, not a one."

Bert stared myopically at the bill still wedged between his swollen knuckles. "Ten dollars!"

"That's right."

Bert jumped out of his chair like a man whose pants were on fire. "Hot damn!" he shouted, leaving his dog behind as he shot into the saloon.

Austin hurried back to the Medicine Lodge Hotel. He raced upstairs, and when he came to Darby's room, he knocked softly. There was no response and he supposed that the Derby Man was asleep. Better not to disturb him.

Austin hurried back downstairs to the registration desk. The clerk raised his eyebrows in question.

"I want to see Ginger," Austin said, lowering his voice.

The clerk winked and leaned in closely. "Of course! When would you like to have her?"

"Why, as soon as possible!"

"You understand that you will need to pay this establishment for her company first."

"Ahhh, yeah," Austin said. "How much?"

The clerk hesitated. "For you, sir, five dollars."

Austin could not help but feel he was being taken advantage of. "I heard it was two."

The clerk showed surprise. "Sir! Two dollars for a woman as lovely and refined as Miss Ginger?"

When Austin remained firm, the clerk said, "Oh, all right. We'll split the difference and you pay three-fifty."

"Very well," Austin said, paying the man. "And tell her to hurry it up."

The clerk smiled discreetly. "Of course."

Austin paced his room for ten minutes before there was a knock on his door. He jumped for the knob and flung the door open.

Ginger was standing in the hall and she was a sight. Bent wrist resting on cocked hip, she wore heavy pancake makeup, a big splash of red lipstick and a dress that left nothing to the imagination. She was smiling and, when Austin took a step backward, she emitted a coarse laugh.

"My, my," she said in a throaty voice as she stepped into the room and closed the door behind her, "if they'd told me that I was going to be visiting such a pretty boy as you, I'd have worn lace garters."

Ginger giggled and Austin gulped. "Ah, Miss Ginger," he said, retreating as the woman advanced to drive him up against his bed. "I think we need to have a little understanding—right now."

She placed her hands on his shoulders and her breath was foul with bad whiskey. She had a musky scent that made Austin's senses reel, and he felt strangely attracted but also repelled.

"Whatever you say, lover man."

"Stop it!" Austin barked.

Ginger froze. The smile went out of her eyes and her voice took on an edge. "Hey now, listen," she snapped, "you sent for me! Not the other way around."

"I wanted to talk to you."

She made a face. "Talk? You wanted to talk to me?"

"Sure."

"Well . . . well, what about?"

"Sit down," Austin said, jumping for a chair. "Would you like a little brandy? It's excellent."

"Why not?"

Austin pulled it out of his coat pocket, eyes casting about for a glass but finding none. "I, ahh . . ."

"Give it to me," she said, tearing the flask from his hand to drain it dry.

Ginger burped and her cheeks flushed. "Now *that,*" she said, tapping the empty flask, "is damned good liquor! Got any more?"

"I'm afraid not."

"What a cryin' shame!" She cocked her head a little sideways, and with her glistening black hair she reminded him of a crow. "So what do you want me to do now?"

"Tell me everything you can about Mrs. Dolly Talbot."

"What!"

"You were her closest childhood friend. I want to know about her."

"Why?" Ginger asked suspiciously.

"It's a long story," Austin said, "and one I doubt you'd find interesting."

"What interests me is money."

"That's what I suspected." Austin drew out a wad of money. "And if you tell me about Dolly, you'll be very well paid."

She stared at the money and licked her lips. "I wish you had some more of that brandy. Ain't you even got any whiskey up here?"

"I'm afraid not."

"I could get killed for talking about Jim's wife."

"You could also earn a lot of money and no one will ever be the wiser. As far as anyone is concerned, this is just a regular visit."

"Dolly came back," Ginger said. "She and Jim stayed here one night. I saw 'em together but they didn't see me. Neither one of them would want to see me."

"Why?"

The woman's ravaged face became pinched. She ran her fingers through her dyed black hair and whispered, "Dolly would feel real bad for me. Jim doesn't want me ever again in his sight. But he sure did when I was young and ripe. Oh, you bet he did! He wanted me all the time."

"But he chose Dolly."

"He *married* Dolly."

Austin's eyes dropped to his hands. It didn't take a very perceptive man to figure out that Ginger had been used by Jim Talbot only to be discarded for Dolly. It didn't take anything to see the bitterness and the pain in Ginger's bloodshot eyes.

"I would have made him a better wife than Dolly. I loved him when I was a girl. Dolly never did. Never!"

"Then why did she marry him?" Austin asked in a gentle voice. "Why, Ginger?"

She almost told him. Austin saw her mouth work silently; then she clamped it shut.

"Ginger, if you won't tell me that, what *can* you tell me about Dolly's past?"

"I could tell you lots about the Talbots. Things that would curl your pretty hair."

Austin waited expectantly. This woman looked to be working herself up. She looked ready to explode with wanting to talk.

"Why don't you start by telling me about Dolly's family?"

"Old man Talbot had both our pa's ambushed." The woman's eyes filled with tears that began to spill over and run down her cheeks, ruining her makeup. "He killed 'em as sure as hell."

"When? Why, Ginger?"

"Long time back. He wanted our homesteads to add to the Rocking T Ranch. Then someone shot him, and Dolly and I celebrated as if it were our sixteenth birthdays. Later on, Dolly married Jim."

Austin shook his head. "But why would Dolly marry a man whose father killed her father?"

Ginger jumped to her feet. "I can't talk about this anymore!" she cried. "I already said too much. You want to know more, ask her brother."

Austin almost fell over. "Her brother? Dolly has a brother!"

"Sure. A lot of people in these parts have brothers."

Austin intercepted the woman before she could reach the door. "Here. That's twenty dollars. There's twenty more if you tell me what happened to Dolly's brother."

"He was shot," Ginger said. "Shot in the left knee and the right hand. It was a terrible thing the day he came riding into Whiskey Creek."

"Who did it?"

Ginger slipped the twenty down the front of her low-cut dress. "Probably Jim. You see, Frank Beavers had let everyone in Whiskey Creek know he would shoot Jim on sight."

"But he never did."

"No," Ginger said. "After someone put a rifle slug through his knee and his gunhand, he wasn't but half the man he used to be. Couldn't ride without bein' in pain. It broke his spirit."

"Wait until I tell the Derby Man about this."

"The who?"

"The Derby Man. America's number one dime novelist. He's a good friend of mine. We're traveling together."

"Has he got money, too?" Ginger asked, suddenly perking up.

"Yes, but he loves Dolly."

"Poor fool," Ginger said. "Everyone loves someone who loves someone else. You know what I mean?"

"I think so. You still love Jim Talbot, don't you?"

"I hate him!"

Austin sighed. "But you also love him and I'm sorry."

Ginger almost broke down. "I'm nothing anymore but I never lost hope. I stayed with Jim for years after Dolly left him. I kept hoping we'd get married, hoping he'd love me enough to take me to wife. But he wouldn't. Sometimes we'd get drunk together and he'd promise to get a preacher and be married. But there was never a preacher within fifty miles, and by the time we got to one, Jim would be sober and mean again."

"Why don't you leave Whiskey Creek?" Austin asked. "Like Dolly."

Ginger shook her head. "Dolly left a long, long time back. She was still real young and men would kill for her, damn her anyway! She's *still* pretty and me, I look like an old hag!"

Austin pulled his silk handkerchief from his pocket. "No, you don't. You're just worn out from bitterness. Maybe if you left and got a fresh start, life would become sweet again. There are plenty of men who would marry you."

"Don't lie to me," she whispered.

He used the handkerchief to dry her tears. "I'm not lying. Go far away where your past means nothing. Start over clean. Come up with a story that will be believed and then live it as though it really happened."

She sniffled. "I . . . I wouldn't know how to act like a respectable woman. What to say or how to behave. Look at me!"

"Buy a lady's clothes. Get your hair fixed properly. Act respectable and if you work hard at it, you'll soon *be* respectable. Change your name and become a lady."

She laughed, but now it was a nice laugh without a trace of coarseness. "Mister, I don't know who you think you are, but you're a real spellbinder and you have a rich imagination."

"I'm a writer—or at least I hope to be one someday soon."

"Life ain't no fairy tale."

Austin knew he might regret it later, but he pulled out two hundred dollars from his pocket. "Here," he said, "take this and buy yourself a new life."

She stared at the money. Her eyes began to fill up again. "But . . ."

He opened the door. "There's a train leaving for Reno in a few days. Be on it! Get out of Whiskey Creek and find a good, hardworking man to marry and take care of until you're both old."

"And you think I could live such a bald-faced lie the rest of my days?"

Austin sighed. "Your past wouldn't even matter to a good man after a short while."

Ginger flung her arms around Austin's neck and hugged him with all of her might. "I *am* leaving!" she choked.

"Good." He pulled her arms from his neck. "I wish you well."

"Mister, about Dolly's brother."

"Yes?"

"He's the gunsmith. He owns that saddle and gun shop

in town but he's only there half the time. Most of the time he stays by himself at his cabin."

"I saw him!"

"He's a bitter man. I don't think he'll even talk to you."

"It's worth a try," Austin said. "Thank you—and good luck!"

She threw her arms around his neck again and this time she kissed him full on the mouth. Her breath was terrible but he waited and let her be the one who pulled away.

"I'm sorry about your friend the Derby Man being in love with Dolly," Ginger said. "And I'm sorry we didn't meet a long time ago so you could have seen me when I was young and pretty."

Austin nodded. "So am I," he said before he closed the door.

Darby sat gazing out of his upstairs hotel room window at the impressive Laramie Mountains. At the moment he had no particular thought in his mind save the sharp realization that, at times, he very much missed New York City. He'd had a fine apartment at 117 Plaza Street and it was filled with books of every size and description. Darby's reading interests were quite varied. He enjoyed horticulture, the arts, and most of all, history. His favorite poet was Robert Burns, closely followed by his own slightly deranged but obviously gifted uncle, Rob Roy Buckingham. Rob Roy would never be anyone else's favorite poet and his doggerel would not stand the test of time. However, in the Irish pubs of Boston, Rob Roy was hailed and freely toasted as America's finest poet.

New York City had been Darby's home for more than a decade after he'd retired as that city's undisputed bare-knuckle champion. There had been some—including Uncle Rob Roy—who'd thought it beneath Darby's dignity to go on to become a circus strongman. But Darby had never been one to listen to any but his own heart and mind. He'd toured with the circus, each year lifting heavier weights and staging more extravagant performances.

His favorite feat had been to lift a girl and her circus pony overhead and then toss them into the air. He always caught the girl before she landed. Unfortunately, the uncooperative pony had chosen on one occasion to relieve itself on Darby, forever ending that unique act. And yes, to Darby's further mortification, Uncle Rob Roy had been in the audience.

"Mr. Buckingham?"

"Come in!" Darby called. "The door isn't locked."

Austin, flushed with excitement, stepped into the room. Darby thought that curious because there was nothing in Whiskey Creek that could possibly excite any man save the two-dollar girl who was probably even now lurking about the dimmest corridors of this shabby hotel.

"Mr. Buckingham! You won't believe what I've discovered!"

"I'm not sure that I even want to know."

"I found out that Dolly's brother is the town gunsmith! I met him in his shop."

"She has a brother?"

"Oh, yes," Austin said, striding across the room. "And there's much more."

"I'm not sure that I want to hear it."

"You *should* hear it!" Austin took a chair. "Listen, I learned that Miss Beavers's father was ambushed and killed by her future father-in-law!"

Darby had come to his feet. "You can't be serious."

"Of course, I'm serious. And Dolly's brother was also ambushed."

"Wait a minute! Wait a minute! You just told me he's the town gunsmith!"

"He is," Austin said, so excited that he had to will himself to slow down. "Apparently, he had issued a challenge to Jim Talbot. He wanted to meet the man here in the street and have a gundown."

"A shoot-out," Darby said. "That's what it's called. Or a gunfight. Either one, but never a gundown."

Austin waved his hand distractedly. "No matter. The point is that Dolly's brother is alive and in town right now!"

Darby reached for his coat and derby. "Let's go see the man and get to the bottom of this affair."

Austin nodded happily. He could see fire in Darby's black eyes again.

"I've got to warn you," Austin said, hurrying down the stairs after Darby and across the lobby of the Medicine Lodge Hotel. "This Frank Beavers is bitter and angry."

"You said something about him being ambushed?"

"Yes," Austin replied. "That's what I was told by . . ."

"No more names," Darby clipped. "I'm confused enough at the moment but we'll get it all cleared up when we meet Dolly's brother. Does he bear any resemblance to Dolly?"

"I don't know. I've never seen Dolly, remember?"

Of course, Darby thought, rushing out the door.

When they arrived at the combination saddle and gun shop, however, the door was locked and shuttered. "Blast!" Darby swore.

"It's almost noon. Maybe he's having a beer and something to eat at one of the saloons."

"Let's go see," Darby said, reversing direction and heading for the saloon.

Bert's dog had moved inside and was gobbling pickled eggs while Bert chugged beer and chewed sloshy tobacco which he used to drench the sawdust floor. There were just two other customers, neither of them the gunsmith.

"Hey, Bert!" Austin called. "I want you to meet the Derby Man!"

Bert popped a pickled egg into his mouth and squinted at Darby. "He dresses just like you, young fella. Older and fatter, though."

Darby scowled but before he could get angry, Austin said, "Where is Frank Beavers's cabin?"

"About five miles to the northwest up on Cherry Creek. Can't miss it."

"Thanks."

As Darby moved outside he growled, "I just knew we'd have to ride those blasted jugheads before we left Wyoming."

"I got a feeling that you're going to fall in love with old Hallelujah," Austin said with a smirk on his handsome face.

"Don't bet on it," Darby said sourly. "In truth, I never met a horse I liked."

Austin squelched a grin. He had read many, many accounts of the Derby Man's intense dislike for horses and horseback riding. The comical descriptions of the Derby Man at a high lope were not to be believed.

"Tell you what," Austin said as they approached the livery where their Reno horses were waiting. "If you'll teach me how to fight Western-style, I'll teach you how to ride a horse."

"Impossible on both counts."

"But why?"

"I'll never be a horseman," Darby said, "and, until you gain weight and strength, you'll never be a formidable fighter."

"Then I'll get strong. You can teach me how to do that."

"I'm not sure that you're willing to pay the price. Putting on weight is all pleasure—if the food and drink are good. But putting on muscle, that's another story."

"I want to be like you," Austin said. "But I can't be if every saloon bully in the West beats the hell out of me. So, the way that I figure it, I *have* to get bigger."

Darby nodded but made no comment. All this new information about Miss Dolly had his mind reeling. A brother and a father, both ambushed by the Talbots? Why then had she married Jim Talbot? And why had she gone back to the man if he was such a ruthless scoundrel?

As they marched toward the livery, it seemed to Darby that every time he learned something new, he actually discovered he knew even less than he'd supposed. About Dolly. About life in general. But maybe Frank Beavers was the key to ending all the confusion surrounding Dolly.

Darby hoped so because there was apparently no question that Miss Dolly Beavers was really Mrs. Dolly Talbot. And while curiosity made Darby determined to unravel this mystery to its bitter end, the pain in his heart made him equally determined to catch the westbound Union Pacific and try to forever erase from memory this place called Whiskey Creek.

SIX

THE PALOMINO was full of vinegar, and it wanted to buck the moment Austin swung his leg over the saddle. Anticipating this behavior, he had tied the reins together and dropped them over his saddlehorn so that the horse could not get its head down. Consequently, the big handsome animal could only crow-hop around the livery yard a few times before settling down.

Darby's new horse, Hallelujah, waited stoically until he jammed his shoe in the stirrup. At that point, however, Hallelujah started off at a trot.

"Stop!" the Derby Man bellowed, hopping frantically along on his right foot while trying to rein the horse up short. "Halt!"

Hallelujah had his own plans, and if Austin had not galloped up and grabbed the sorrel by the bit, the animal would probably have dragged Darby all the way back to Nevada.

"Easy," Austin said, getting the horse under control.

"Preacher's horse, my foot!" Darby snorted, swinging his right leg over the cantle and wedging himself into the seat. It was too snug, of course. Every saddle he'd ever ridden was made for the skinny haunches of a working cowboy.

"Your saddle is too small and your stirrups are too long," Austin said.

"The hell with them! Let's ride out."

"No," Austin said, dismounting. "I can't enlarge your saddle but it's senseless to gall the insides of your legs just because we didn't take a minute to adjust the stirrups."

Darby grumbled but was grateful. He'd had a few terrible saddle sores since beginning his western adventures.

"I expect," Austin was saying as he quickly unlaced the stirrup leathers and shortened them, "that I'll have a few galls myself. I'm sure not used to these western saddles. English is my style."

"You'll come to appreciate them," Darby said, "about the time that you need to grab a saddlehorn."

"I suppose."

Austin finished making the adjustments. "You might want to take it a little slowly on old Hallelujah here until you two become better acquainted."

"Excellent advice. Do you suppose we might even teach the beast that it is not supposed to trot off until I am completely in the saddle?"

"We can work on that."

"Perhaps," Darby said hopefully, "I won't ever have to ride him again and it really won't be necessary."

When Austin shook his head and remounted the flashy palomino, Darby felt a twinge of envy. Austin, tall, lean and erect, looked wonderful on horseback while Darby knew he rode with all the grace and elegance of an overstuffed sack of potatoes. Darby forced his eyes to the front. The palomino wanted to run but Austin held it to a walk and they kept that slow but satisfying pace for the next hour and a half.

Cherry Creek didn't have a creek, just the hint of a sandy wash. There was, however, a fine mountain spring up in the pines and it flowed into a large meadow. Frank's log cabin was situated at the east end of the meadow atop a rocky knoll where he had a full-circle view for a half mile in any direction.

"You'll notice," Darby said, "that no one could get within rifle range of that cabin without being seen."

Austin nodded. "Frank was sitting at his bench when I saw him in his shop so I didn't notice a limp. However, I do recall that he was wearing thin leather gloves, which struck me as odd."

"If he took a rifle bullet in his gunhand, chances are that those gloves protect tender scar tissue."

"I suppose so," Austin agreed. "Maybe that's why the man has such a foul disposition."

"If you'd taken two rifle slugs in ambush and your father had been shot down in cold blood," Darby said, "then I guess you'd be a little embittered, too."

"Good point," Austin conceded as he surveyed the little homestead. "That sure isn't much of a cabin, is it?"

Austin was right. The sagging one-room cabin looked ready to collapse. It didn't even have glass windows, and the only indication that it had not been abandoned was a big mule that began to bray a loud greeting as it trotted back and forth in its pole corral.

"Do you suppose he rides that ugly thing?" Austin asked.

"Wouldn't surprise me. A lot of men prefer them over horses because they're smarter and they're more surefooted on a narrow mountain trail."

"Well," Austin said, patting the neck of his fine palomino, "I'd never ride one of those overgrown jackrabbits."

"You would if you had to," Darby said. "But right now . . ."

Darby's words were interrupted by the roar of a huge buffalo rifle and his derby spun crazily into the air. "Holy hominy!" he shouted as Hallelujah wheeled around and took off running with the bit clamped firmly in his teeth.

Austin was right behind them; because the palomino was faster, Austin managed to overtake the Derby Man's runaway horse, grab the reins and help him drag the animal to a standstill.

"Blast!" Darby shouted, piling off Hallelujah and glaring

back at the cabin to see a short, stocky man reloading a long rifle.

"Is that him?"

Austin studied the figure. "That's Frank Beavers, all right."

"Hey!" Darby shouted, starting back. "We come in peace! We want to talk to you."

"Go away, whoever you are!"

Darby kept walking forward. Surely this fool would be reasonable enough at least to hear him out. "I'm the Derby Man! I was supposed to marry your sister, Dolly!"

Darby waited a moment. When there was no response he called out again. "I know your sister is in trouble. We want to help her!"

"Ain't no use! Go away!"

Darby kept walking. "I'm coming in!"

"You're a mighty big target. First bullet was a warning. The next will put you underground."

Austin swallowed. "Maybe we ought to listen to him. I don't think he's bluffing, Mr. Buckingham!"

But Darby wasn't listening. "Here," he said, stopping for a moment to hand his reins to Austin. "If the fool does drill me, see that justice is served."

"But . . ."

"Please, just do it." Darby drew a cigar from his pocket and lit it. He inhaled deeply and then said, "I don't think this man is a killer. He's Dolly's own flesh and blood."

"That doesn't mean anything!"

Darby wasn't listening as he started forward again, eyes fixed on the man and his rifle. He did not go twenty yards before Frank raised the big Sharps rifle to his shoulder and yelled, "That's far enough!"

But the Derby Man ignored the warning. This man was Dolly's brother and Darby was betting that Frank Beavers wasn't any more capable of murder than Dolly would be under similar circumstances.

"I said, that's far enough!" Frank hollered.

Darby did not slow his stride but he could not help flinching when the powerful rifle boomed again and he felt a heavy slug whistle past his left ear.

"Damn you!" Frank screamed, frantically trying to reload as Darby broke into a run.

Frank was an expert, but in an emergency and once he achieved some momentum, Darby moved very fast for a big man. Arms and legs pistoning, breath burning, he watched as the man frantically reloaded.

Just as Frank was lifting his rifle, Darby's arm swept up and knocked it skyward. The rifle belched smoke and fire and Darby grabbed Frank and shook him until his head flopped back and forth and the rifle spilled to the ground.

"What the deuce is the matter with you!" Darby roared. "I come to help your sister and you threaten to shoot me? Are you crazy?"

"Let go of me!"

Darby shoved the man away. "I want some answers from you," he said, fists balled, chest heaving for breath.

"I know what you two really are! You're Jim Talbot's friends!"

"What gives you that ridiculous idea?"

"Well just look at the way you're dressed! You're not cowboys. You're Eastern money people. Talbot is the only man in these parts that has that kind of friends. And the liveryman in Whiskey Creek told me that your young friend was askin' directions to the Rocking T Ranch! You wouldn't go there unless you were Talbot's friend."

"Wrong on all counts," Darby wheezed, still trying to catch his wind. "I was engaged to marry your sister. She was supposed to meet me at Promontory Point in Utah. It was to be a historic and happy celebration. All the arrangements were made for the nuptials and then she vanished. We traced her here. Now, all that's left is for you to tell me *why* she went back to Jim Talbot."

Frank Beavers seemed to deflate. "Mister," he said after a long pause, "I'm afraid that my sister has gone crazy."

Darby took a menacing step forward. "Don't ever say that again to me or I'll tear your head off—brother or no brother."

"Well, how else can you explain it!" Frank exclaimed. "As far as I know, she's still married to Jim Talbot. So *you* tell me how my sister was supposed to be married to two men at the same time."

Darby's voice softened. "Listen, I'm sorry we got crossways of each other. I presume that we both want to help Dolly. Is that true?"

"Sure," Frank whispered. "She's my sister and I hate Jim Talbot."

"Fair enough. So, after I tell you what I know, why don't you fill in some of the blanks and then maybe we can sort things out."

Frank listened, his face bitter as Darby quickly ran over the facts as he understood them. Old James Talbot had been ambushed and killed but not before he'd killed Frank and Dolly's father. Dolly had married Jim Talbot. Then Dolly had vanished from Whiskey Creek.

"Is all that true?"

"Yeah," Frank said. "Old James Talbot had our pa ambushed."

"Did you ambush Talbot?"

"I wanted to," Frank said. "And I've wished every day since that I had. But I didn't. Jim blamed me, of course; in those days, I was pretty hot-blooded."

"But why did she marry Jim Talbot in the first place?" Darby asked.

"Maybe you better ask Dolly."

"I will. But right now, I'm asking you."

Frank's mouth crimped. "I ain't makin' excuses for my only sister but she was real young then. The Talbots already had money, land, cattle and power—we had nothing but hard times. After our pa was ambushed, I'd let it be known that I'd draw down old James or young Jim, whichever I met first."

"But that never happened, did it?" Austin said.

"No," Frank Beavers said with bitterness. "Like my pa, I was ambushed by some sharpshooter up in the trees. I was hikin' across that meadow yonder. First bullet caught me in the hand. I started runnin' for this cabin and took another slug in the knee. I went right down and it was all I could do to keep from bleeding to death."

Darby frowned. "Why do you suppose the ambusher didn't finish you off?"

"I got myself down in a low spot so I couldn't be seen. Then, too," Frank said, "I was packing a six-gun and, even left-handed, I would have been big trouble. I guess Jim Talbot figured that I wasn't worth the risk. I've thought about it a hundred times. Often wished he had killed me and then I get mad all over again and make up my mind to kill him."

"What chance would you have?" Darby asked.

"Even left-handed, I'm still one of the finest marksmen in this part of Wyoming," Frank clipped. "I could have put both bullets through your chest, Buckingham."

Darby bristled. "You did manage to ruin my derby!"

"Better than airing a hole in your fool head," Frank retorted. "On the second shot, I was just tryin' to nip your ear enough to make you lose your nerve and turn tail."

"You failed."

"Yeah," Frank said, "but I was playing it safe. And I'll by God bet you heard the slug whine as it passed."

"I did," Darby admitted.

"I can hit what I aim for."

"Then why haven't you shot Jim Talbot?"

Frank's expression grew bleak. "I don't know," he said in a quiet voice. "I've been asking myself that question for twenty years. Always in pain, always twisted up in the guts with hate. I . . . I dunno. Maybe it's just that I ain't got enough heart."

"And you haven't seen your sister since she came back?"

"No. Talbot wouldn't allow that."

"Exactly what is his hold on her after all these years?" Darby demanded.

A hard mask slipped over the man's face. "You'll have to ask her that question."

"I will."

"Do that, but if you cross onto Rocking T land, Jim Talbot will have you shot for trespassing," Frank warned. "My guess is he's got people in Whiskey Creek, Laramie and Cheyenne watching to see if you come for my sister."

"In that case," Darby said, "we'll just have to find a way to take him by surprise."

"I'm going with you to the Rocking T Ranch," Frank announced. "There'll be a gunfight. I want to be in on it."

Darby frowned. "Maybe you just *want* a gunfight so you can either kill Jim Talbot or have him kill you. I'd like to think that we can do this without anyone dying."

"So would I," Austin seconded.

Frank scoffed out loud. "You gents don't know Talbot like I do! He had Dolly once and he's not the kind of man to let go of anything. And Lord help the man who tries to take something from him."

Darby said, "And I suppose he's got quite a few gunmen on his payroll?"

"Five or six. Top gunnies who'd kill you both without battin' an eye."

"Mr. Buckingham," Austin said after a long silence, "it wouldn't hurt to let this man come along. We could sure use someone who knows this country in case we have to run and hide."

Before Darby could answer, Frank said, "Without me, you'll never get within sight of the ranch house. You'll never see my sister's face."

Darby believed the man. He and Austin were determined and courageous but they were no match for professional gunfighters.

"Can I make a suggestion?" Frank said.

Darby's chin dipped in assent. "Let's hear it."

"My guess is that Jim Talbot does have a man watching out for you in Whiskey Creek. Best thing to do would be to get on the westbound train and make Talbot think that you gave up and returned to Nevada. Then we can double back and strike out for the Rocking T and catch Talbot and his men off guard."

"That's not a bad idea," Austin said hopefully. "That way, we can gain the critical element of surprise."

Darby clenched his fists. "But the train doesn't leave for two more days!"

"We'll have only one chance to do this," Austin said.

Darby stifled his anger. They were right, of course. But, oh, how it grated him to wait even an hour longer than necessary to see Dolly Beavers again and to find out what terrible hold Talbot had on her.

"All right," he said at last. "We'll play a charade, pretend to sell our horses and return to Reno. And I presume, Mr. Beavers, you will be waiting somewhere between Whiskey Creek and Laramie for us?"

"I got just the place in mind where you can jump off. It's a grade where the train slows down to damn near a walk."

"Sounds perfect."

"It will be," Frank said. "We'll time it to hit the Rocking T at night and then we'll settle this once and for all."

Darby didn't like what he heard in Frank's voice. The man was obviously twisted with bitterness and could not be trusted. Once he saw Jim Talbot, Frank would open fire and consequences be damned.

"I don't like any of this," Darby said, "but it's the only chance we've got of reaching Miss Beavers."

"Can either of you shoot?" Frank asked.

"I can," Austin declared.

"Before you ride back to Whiskey Creek, we'll see about that." Frank turned to Darby. "What about you?"

"I got a double-barreled shotgun in my hotel room,"

Darby growled. "I just point it in the general direction I mean to hit, then pull the trigger."

Frank shook his head, but something he saw in Darby Buckingham's face made him decide to keep his mouth shut.

SEVEN

DARBY AND AUSTIN arrived back in Whiskey Creek soon after dark. They had a quick dinner of steak and potatoes washed down with watery beer; then each retired to his room.

Darby slept better that night, even though the discoveries he'd made concerning Dolly were deeply troubling. He could understand why she had married Jim Talbot when she was young, poor and impressionable. What he could not understand was why she had returned to Whiskey Creek and allowed herself to become ensnared in Talbot's web after so many years of freedom. Was it simply that she had thought she had to get a divorce from the Wyoming rancher before she could become Darby's wife? And if that most obvious reason was entirely responsible for her disappearance, why hadn't she confided in Darby so that they could handle this legal entanglement together? Had she so little trust in his love that she thought an error in her youth could not be forgiven? Darby hoped not. He had thought they had no secrets, no reservations, no limitations to their trust. This really hurt, far more than if Dolly had confided her dark secret of a past marriage.

Darby kept his disappointment well hidden during the next two restless days as they waited for the westbound Union Pacific to roll into Whiskey Creek. If Jim Talbot did have a spy watching them, Darby never saw evidence of his presence.

"We are returning to Reno," he told everyone he met. "It was a mistake to come. We sold our horses and saddles to the livery."

"Tell me, Mr. Buckingham, why *did* you come?" the bartender asked.

"For our health and the beauty of this Laramie Mountain country," Darby replied, breathing in deeply as if inhaling the pine-scented air. "For the pure vigor and inspiration of Wyoming."

The bartender had not been able to stifle a yawn. "You think *this* is invigorating? You should have seen it when the Union Pacific work crews were in town! I tell you, this saloon was packed night and day. We had hurdy-gurdy girls and the liquor flowed like a river rushin' down to the sea. This town will never see such exciting times again, Mr. Buckingham. Never."

"If you feel that way about it," Darby said, "then why don't you leave?"

"Where would I go? I don't have the cash to tear down and haul this saloon over to Laramie or Cheyenne where I could make some real money. And I can't sell the damned place because business is so bad. So here I am, stuck for the rest of my natural life."

"It isn't worth your life," Darby tried to explain. "A man should do what he wants to do." He lit a cigar and leaned on the bar. "Tell me the truth," he said, "if you could do exactly what you wanted to do at this very minute, what would it be?"

The bartender, a round-faced Irishman named O'Brien, pursed his lips thoughtfully. "Well, sir, I guess I'd like to be drinkin' French champagne with a couple of those hurdy-gurdy girls bouncin' up and down on each of my knees."

Darby blinked. "That's it? That's what you'd do if you could choose *anything?*"

O'Brien shrugged. "Sure! Why not!"

Darby blew a smoke ring and hid his disappointment well. "Perhaps," he said, turning away, "this *is* exactly where you belong."

He went outside and found Austin sitting with Bert. The old man was spinning stories about mustanging days.

"We used to mustang some down in Nevada where you gentlemen come from. Used to do pretty good, too. It was damned rough country, though. Only way to catch mustangs in the desert is to fence off their water holes. Sooner or later, wild horses got to come in for a drink and then you got 'em."

"How?" Austin asked. "How have you got 'em?"

"Well, you just hire a Paiute Injun to hide in a little hole by the gate. When the mustangs finally go inside the corral, the Injun jumps out like a flea offa a burnin' skillet and pops the gate shut!" Bert grinned. "Course, if he trips or is a mite slow getting the gate shut, well sir, he's brown mush, 'cause them mustangs will stomp right back over the top of him."

"I see," Austin said, furiously taking notes.

"Ahh-hem," Darby coughed. "Mr. Applegate, why don't we see how good you are with that new Winchester that we got in Reno?"

"Excellent idea!"

"You pilgrims be careful now," Bert called as they were leaving. "Wouldn't surprise me nor the other folks around here if you greenhorns accidentally shot yourselves to death."

Darby ignored the remark but Austin just laughed. After getting their weapons, they walked half a mile out of Whiskey Creek and found a good shooting spot.

"I'll line up some small rocks on that big boulder," Austin said. "We can shoot at them for practice."

Darby nodded. In his fist was his trusty double-barreled shotgun. In his pocket was a pearl-handled .45 caliber derringer. He wasn't worth a damn with either weapon but he'd had to use them a time or two since coming to the West and they hadn't failed him.

After the rocks were in place, Austin took up his Winchester, levered a shell into the breech and said, "From the left."

"What . . ."

Austin's answer was with his rifle. His first shot exploded a rock, and before the rolling thunder of the retort had died into the nearby hills, another rock exploded. Then another and another. He missed only one of seven.

"What remarkably good shooting!" Darby exclaimed. "You said you knew how to handle firearms, but I never suspected that you were *that* good."

Austin lowered his rifle. "Back east, we did a lot of hunting on my father's estate."

"What did you shoot?" Darby asked.

"Mostly game birds, some deer."

"I hope," Darby said, "you aren't forced to shoot men."

"Me, too," Austin said.

Darby raised his shotgun, took aim and pulled both triggers. The blast was deafening. A huge cloud of black smoke poured from the barrels, and when it cleared, Darby grinned. "See, no rock."

"Almost no boulder, either," Austin said. "Have you ever *cleaned* that weapon?"

"No. But I don't fire it but once in a great while."

"May I?" Austin asked, holding out his hands.

"Of course."

Austin inspected both barrels. They were filthy. "Mr. Buckingham," he said, "why don't you let me clean this shotgun tonight? It could save your life and mine as well."

"If you wish," Darby said, shrugging his powerful shoulders. "I just assumed that any debris in the barrels would be blown out after each discharge."

"Not exactly," Austin told him.

Darby turned on his heel, jammed his hands into his pockets and walked away without comment, head down, short legs moving with purpose. Austin knew that posture signified Darby's thoughts were again occupied by Dolly Beavers and the newfound discovery of her troubled past. Austin realized how hard it was for Darby to wait so that they could pull off the ruse of returning to Nevada. Everything in the man clamored to rush to Dolly's aid.

Given Darby's anxiety, their brief stay in Whiskey Creek passed very slowly; when the time finally came for them to catch their train, they were both tense. They had not seen Frank Beavers since the day they'd left his cabin and he'd drawn them a map of where he would be waiting when they jumped from the train.

"There's a long grade about five miles to the west of town," Frank had explained. "You'll pass a stand of lightning-burned trees on your right and it'll come up right after that. The train will have to slow way down and you can hop off the caboose without breaking your legs."

"Are you sure?"

"Course I'm sure!" Frank had snapped. "And I'll be waitin' in those trees with your horses."

At the time, the plan had seemed reasonable and good. But now, as they bought their tickets and waited for the train to pull into the station, Darby was having second thoughts. "Maybe we should have checked with Frank Beavers this morning to make sure that he has everything straight."

"I wouldn't worry about it."

"Well, I *am* worried," Darby said. "We'll be in a real mess if we jump the train and he's not there."

The Derby Man consulted his pocket watch. "The train is always late. Would you mind hurrying over to see if he's at his shop?"

"All right," Austin said. "I'll be back in less than five minutes."

Darby watched the young man hurry away. It was probably foolishness on his part to ask Austin to double-check, but Frank Beavers was not the kind of man who instilled great confidence. He was like a bomb, wired and ready to explode. Darby was not at all sure what was going to happen at the Rocking T Ranch, but he would have to watch Frank every minute or the man would get them all killed because of his lust for revenge.

"Well, hello there! May I join you?" a sensuous voice purred.

Darby glanced up and then did a double take. A woman about his own age was eying him like a cat would a fat mouse. She licked her lips. Darby gulped. The woman had coal-black hair arranged in the latest style and was dressed respectably enough, but she was so predatory she made him squirm.

"Ahh," he stammered, "I'm—I'm with someone."

"Your wife?"

He could not quite bring himself to tell the expedient lie. "No. Just a friend."

"Well, then," she said, extending a gloved hand, "my name is *Miss* Dora Puddingstone. And yours, sir?"

"Darby Buckingham."

"Pleasure to meet you, I'm sure," she said, batting her eyes. "My, but isn't this exciting!"

"What?"

"Taking this long railroad ride together!" she said, breathing whiskey fumes in his face as she plunked down beside him.

Darby scooted along the bench. "Uh . . . yes. It certainly is."

"Do you live in Nevada, Mr. Buckingham?"

"Is that where you're going, Miss Puddingstone?"

"I'm not entirely sure." She scooted closer. "You see, my husband died just recently and so I'm sort of . . . well . . . alone in this big cruel world. I wish I had a big, strong man like you to watch over me, Mr. Buckingham."

"Uh . . ." Darby gulped again. Forward women had always made him uneasy. "I'm sure you'll find someone. Out west there is never a shortage of men or mosquitos."

"Well put!" she cried, placing her hand on his knee. "Are you a man of letters?"

"Words, Miss Puddingstone. I write dime novels."

"Oh hell!" she said angrily. "Why didn't you just come right out and say that you were the Derby Man!"

"Beg your pardon?"

"Never mind. Austin told me all about you and Dolly. Speaking of which, where is that handsome young man?"

"He'll be back momentarily. Who are you?"

She leaned close and whispered. "My real name isn't Miss Puddingstone."

"It isn't?"

"No. I'm Ginger! Didn't he ever tell you about me?"

Darby blushed. "Why yes, but . . ."

"Don't tell a soul, though," she ordered, casting her eyes about for fresh prey. Then, spotting another single and promising man, Ginger bounced to her feet, put on her smile and sashayed across the train station. A moment later and just as the westbound Union Pacific pulled into the station, Austin came rushing up.

"Did you locate Frank?" Darby asked with concern.

"No," Austin said, "but I ran over to the livery and our horses are gone. I'm sure that Frank has them and is waiting right now just where he's supposed to be."

"I hope you're right," Darby said, watching the woman who'd accosted him link her arm through that of her second victim as they boarded the train. "By the way, who is that woman?"

Austin followed Darby's eyes. "Why, that's Ginger. She looks terrific! You wouldn't believe she's the same woman I saw a couple of days ago in my hotel room. She's Whiskey Creek's 'two-dollar woman'—the one who told me about Dolly having a brother."

Darby's face registered surprise, but only for an instant. Then he boarded the train and was recognized immediately by the conductor. "Why, Mr. Buckingham, what a surprise to have you back on board! You shouldn't be sitting in our coach car. Come on up to the first class car where the gentlemen belong!"

Darby wanted to be near the back of the train so that they would not be seen as they jumped. "This is just fine. We'll change cars later," Darby said, forcing a tight smile.

"Whatever you say, sir," the conductor said with a shake of his head as he moved up the aisle.

"Regrettably, I hurt the man's feelings," Darby remarked.

"It's nothing compared to what he'll go through when he discovers we are missing."

"I hadn't thought about that," Darby said, scowling. "You don't suppose they'd stop the train and back it down the line in search of me, do you?"

"No," Austin said, "I don't. Not even you rate that kind of inconvenience. The train does have a schedule."

"Good point," Darby conceded as the steam whistle blasted and their train gathered momentum.

They sat anxiously beside the window for several minutes; then they abandoned their seats and slipped out to the platform between their coach and the caboose.

"We ought to be approaching that stand of blistered pines any minute now," Darby said, gripping the rail and leaning so far out that he almost lost his balance and toppled over the rail.

"Blast!"

"What?"

"There isn't a stand of timber as far as the eye can see, which must be twenty miles!" Darby cried. "Take a look for yourself!"

Austin did take a look. With Darby hanging onto his coattails, he leaned out and saw that the Derby Man was correct.

"Maybe Frank was confused and it's on the *other* side of the train."

Darby rushed across the platform and they repeated the

exercise. Austin was hauled back onto the platform. "No trees and no grade on either side."

"We've been bamboozled!" Darby cried. "That lying scoundrel tricked us into leaving Whiskey Creek!"

"But why?"

"How should I know! Maybe both Beavers are crazy."

"Well, what are we going to do? The train is gathering speed."

Darby cussed. The locomotive answered with a long, shrill whistle.

"Oh, the hell with it!" Darby shouted as he threw himself over the platform's rail.

Austin saw the Derby Man hang in the air for an instant, then drop, hit the steep railroad bed and go tumbling end over end until the poor man came to a rest in the prairie grass. This was Austin's moment of truth. Either he jumped, too—or he allowed the Derby Man, and his own dream of becoming America's next great dime novelist, pass from his life forever.

Austin jumped and Darby watched his young friend silhouetted against the smoke and sky before he fell. He saw Austin strike the railroad bed, then somersault into a huge boulder.

"Uh-oh," Darby said, pushing himself to his feet and wiping cinders from his clothes before hurrying over to Austin.

"Mr. Applegate! Can you hear me?"

Austin didn't hear anything. He was knocked out cold. Darby felt his pulse and it was strong. He found Austin's derby and jammed it down tightly on the man's head, then picked Austin up and slung him over his shoulder.

Darby had just two choices—either head for Frank Beavers's log cabin, or return to Whiskey Creek. Darby's face was black with anger and he muttered something to himself as he headed for the miserable little cabin.

EIGHT

FRANK BEAVERS jammed his Sharps rifle into his saddle boot and mounted his mule, which brayed a farewell to Hallelujah and Austin's palomino gelding. Frank's expression was grim and he kicked the mule in her flanks, saying, "Get along, Milly."

The mule's long ears twitched back and forth like a grasshopper's antennae. It struck off to the north and kept moving steadily for the next five hours up one ridge and then down another, crawling higher into the Laramie Mountains.

Throughout the long afternoon, Frank thought little about Darby and Austin. All his hard thinking was finished now. He'd wrestled with this decision to leave the two Easterners stranded by the railroad tracks and he knew he was doing the right thing by them. Jim Talbot needed killing and Frank figured it was best he did the job alone.

By late afternoon, Frank crossed onto land that once had belonged to his family, land that his father had been murdered for and that would never belong to him, but might pass on to Dolly. The idea that Dolly could possibly become heir to the Rocking T Ranch brought a tight smile of satisfaction to Frank's lips.

Two hours before sunset, Frank dismounted in an old grove of cottonwood and aspen. He tied up the mule and picked his way through heavy underbrush until he came to the blackened ruins of what had once been his family's cabin. The only thing now standing was the rock fireplace he'd helped his father build when he was just a little shaver. Everything else was gone, picked over by Talbot's cowboys who used the fireplace for their campfire. They'd desecrated the old Beavers homestead with rusty tin cans and smashed whiskey bottles.

Frank's left knee was throbbing so fiercely that he could hardly walk. He sat down on a fallen log and cradled his chin in his cupped hands. He closed his pain-stricken eyes and summoned up a fading vision of a time long ago, when he and Dolly had played in this stand of young trees. Somewhere among these trees, their names were carved.

Those had been lean but happy years, the only really good ones Frank had ever known. Sure, there had always been the ominous threat of James Talbot, hungering to gobble up more range. But Frank's pa had worked hard and even scrimped together enough money each year to take them on a shopping trip to Denver. And someday, he'd told them, they'd all become prosperous enough to look even rich old James Talbot in the eye.

All that had changed with the single crash of an ambusher's rifle on the day Frank's father had died. A few months later, when Frank had come upon old man Talbot chasing one of their cows out of a nearby ravine, revenge had been damned sweet. Everyone knew that he'd killed Talbot, but Frank had never admitted it to a soul, not even to Dolly.

Frank massaged his knee with his good hand. As he rubbed the shattered kneecap, he shifted his focus to Jim Talbot. Too bad he'd never been able to catch the man riding this range all alone. Too bad, because now he was going to have to sneak into Rocking T headquarters and kill Talbot in his own damned bed.

Frank swallowed. He tried not to think of what he'd do if he found Dolly in that same bed. Maybe . . . maybe, if he did, he'd kill her, too. He knew he was crazy enough to do most any damn thing after all these years of waiting and hating. Frank hobbled painfully back to his mule, then stifled a groan as he shoved his left boot into the stirrup and hauled himself back into the saddle.

"Another hour will do it," he said to the mule as they rode slowly through the trees and into the glow of what he felt sure would be his last sundown.

Frank had no difficulty skirting the ranch and moving down a ridge to the edge of the ranchyard. The lights in the big house blazed and he could hear conversation punctuated by intermittent laughter. Frank eased his right leg over his cantle and dismounted. "Milly, if you start brayin' at those horses, I'll slit your throat."

Milly stamped wearily and raised her head, intent on the ranch horses. Frank knew she was going to bray so he untied his rope and put a choke knot under Milly's gullet that made it impossible for her to do anything other than breathe. The mule didn't understand and rolled her eyes with distress. Frank paid her no mind. She'd settle down, and come morning some cowboy would find her and untie the painful knot. Milly was a prize. Anyone with good sense could see that she was a fine, fine animal, worth more than two or even three top cow ponies.

"Who knows," Frank said, "maybe you'll even get to pull Talbot's hearse wagon."

Frank checked the Army Colt on his left hip, knowing it was in perfect working order because he'd cleaned and oiled it the previous afternoon. Right-handed, he'd once been on the level of a professional gunfighter. Left-handed, he was slow but prided himself on being accurate enough to consistently hit a man-sized target at one hundred yards. The .44 caliber Army Colt had originally been percussion but Frank had modified it to accept the new metallic cartridges. His big-bored Sharps rifle had an accuracy range of one thousand yards but it wouldn't do him much good this night. More likely, it'd slow him down too much or he'd bang it on something and give himself away.

Frank hated to do it, but he decided to leave the breechloader with Milly.

"I might make it back," he told the mule. "Otherwise, this is goodbye, old gal."

Milly was angry. She nipped at him but Frank jumped back to avoid the hard snap of her long yellow teeth, and then he moved down through the trees. His main concern was the possibility of being announced by some ranchyard dog but that proved to be a needless worry.

In fifteen minutes he was at the outermost corrals, hobbling painfully from one building to another in an erratic path to the ranch house. Reaching it, he scooted under the porch and came face to face with a big dog that growled from way down in its throat.

"Easy, boy," Frank said, hand slipping to the knife in his boot. "This here space is big enough for us both."

The dog kept growling, and even though it was too dark to see the animal clearly, it sounded huge and mean. But Frank had his knife in his fist now and no dog, not even a full-grown timber wolf, would have driven him out from under Jim Talbot's front porch.

"You just settle down," Frank warned, knife tip pointed toward the animal. "There's going to be enough blood spilled before this night is over without adding yours, too."

The dog growled steadily for another ten minutes, then fell silent. After an hour, Frank suspected that it had moved off to leave him alone. Once, he thought he heard his sister's voice but he couldn't be certain. Mostly though, Frank strained hard to recognize the hated sound of Jim Talbot's voice but he never pinpointed it because the floorboards overhead creaked and groaned constantly, making it impossible to overhear anything except muffled conversation. The hour grew late, and when Frank saw the bunkhouse lights die he decided that he'd wait two more hours just to be on the safe side.

Waiting was hard. Frank closed his eyes and tried to picture how it would be when he got the drop on Jim Talbot. God, he hoped Dolly wasn't in bed with the man!

The ranch house grew silent. Frank thought he heard Milly thrashing around up in the trees and he prayed the mule would not break loose and come charging down into the ranchyard, rousing the cowboys. If they found her, the Rocking T cowboys would instantly recognize Milly and know that Frank Beavers was on the property with murder in his heart. Once that happened, Frank realized that he wouldn't have a snowball's chance in hell of killing Talbot.

Minutes seemed hours but they eventually passed and Frank crawled out from under the porch and eased his weight onto it. He moved to the front door and opened it quietly, then slipped into the room, dragging his Colt out of his holster, feeling sweat beading on his forehead. The entry hall was dark. Upstairs, he could see the dim glow of lamplight and he wasted no time making up his mind to go to it just as directly as a moth to a flame. The stairs were carpeted and made no sound. When he neared the upper landing, Frank paused and held his breath, head whipping first to the right and then to the left.

One door was closed but Frank could see a blade of light etched along its bottom. The other door was ajar and cast a thick wedge of light into the hall.

Which door? Frank asked himself. He decided to try the one that was ajar, and as he tiptoed toward it his heart banged against the insides of his ribs hard enough to drown out every other sound. Clenching his six-gun, he flattened himself against the wall and took a quick peek.

It was Talbot! The rancher was seated behind a big rolltop desk, his back to Frank as he scratched away on a piece of paper with a quill pen. Frank stepped inside, cocking the hammer of his gun.

Jim Talbot heard the ominous metallic sound and swiveled around in his office chair. Recognizing Frank, his jaw dropped; then he clamped his mouth shut.

"This has been a long, long time coming," Frank whispered, "but it was worth the wait."

The quill spilled from Talbot's fist and rolled down his chest, ruining his expensive white silk shirt. Frank enjoyed watching the man's features corrode with raw fear.

"Frank, if you pull that trigger you'll never get out of here alive!"

The remark caused Frank to chuckle softly. "Haven't you guessed that I don't care? You see, my life is all pain and revenge, Jim. I've nothing to lose. But you? Well, look at all you have! Must be pretty hard to stare into the face of death when you own damned near everything, including my sister."

Talbot threw his eyes around the room. Frank had no idea what he was looking for, other than some way out of being killed.

"For the record, I did kill your pa," Frank said happily. "Shot him from ambush just like he did my pa. Only difference was, I shot him in the *belly!* He died real, real hard. He wept like a baby. Begged me to put him out of his misery."

"You sick bastard!"

"I'm going to shoot you in the belly, too," Frank announced. "I'm going to watch you die slow. Bet you'll cry even louder than your pa did."

"You won't live long enough to hear it!" Talbot choked. "My men will come running and you won't last five minutes."

"Probably not," Frank said with a shrug of his shoulders. "But I'll take a few more with me and I'll go out quick."

Talbot licked his lips. "Frank, do you want money—lots of money?"

"No."

"Then what about your old homestead? I can deed it back right now with a letter."

"It's too late."

"Then what is it! Your sister? Is that why you're here?"

Frank shook his head.

"It *must* be Dolly!" the rancher cried. "Is that what this is about after all these years?"

"I said no."

Talbot shouted, "Dolly! Dolly, it's your crazy brother! He's going to kill me!"

The gun in Frank's fist trembled. "This is between you and me!"

"Not anymore, it isn't," Talbot said as they both heard Dolly's door bang open.

"Frank!"

He turned, half in and half out of the doorway, to see Dolly. She was dressed in a red satin nightgown, long blonde hair shining in the lamplight. It looked just like it had when they were kids and their pa brushed it before they were read a story and sent to bed.

"Get back into your room!" Frank commanded.

"Frank, I'm all right," Dolly pleaded. "You shouldn't have come. You'll be killed!"

"It doesn't matter!"

"Talk sense to him!" Talbot shouted from his office chair. "Dolly, tell him you came of your own free will. You're still my wife, tell him to put down that gun!"

Dolly raised her hands in supplication. "Frank," she whispered, "we can still get you out of here alive. There's still a chance if you holster your gun."

"No," he heard himself say.

"Tell him, Dolly!"

"Frank, please! I don't know why you came here, but there's nothing you can do now."

"You're wrong," he said. "I got a crippled hand and a knee that pains me every waking hour. I've no land, no ranch, no pride. Nothing!"

Dolly took another step toward her brother. "This is not the way. Jim will let you go, won't you!"

"Hell, yes! If he puts down the gun, I'll let him go."

"See. You heard him." Dolly was begging. "I don't want to lose you, Frank. You're all the family I have left!"

"I'm sorry but this has to be." Frank tried a smile that was an abysmal failure. "Maybe you'll even inherit the Rocking T. You think of that?"

"I won't."

"Yeah, well, you better get something! He made you marry him. I don't know why, but he did. So it's time he paid."

"Frank," she pleaded, "if only you'd . . ."

Dolly never finished her sentence. She saw her brother suddenly spin around into the doorway and heard the explosion of Talbot's pocket derringer. Her brother staggered backward into the hallway and his pistol emptied a slug into the hallway carpet.

"Frank!" she exclaimed, lunging at him.

Before Dolly could cover the small distance between them, Frank's arms began to windmill and he struck the landing rail. It collapsed and he fell with a rush and a scream. An instant later, Dolly heard the sound of her brother's body hitting the floor below and the muffled retort of his six-gun.

"Frank!" she cried, whirling and racing down the stairs.

He was dead. There was a wet red rose flooding across his chest and his neck was twisted at a terrible angle.

Dolly bent her head and wept bitterly.

"Don't waste your tears on him!" Talbot raged from up on the landing. "Your brother was a walking dead man from the moment he killed my pa!"

Dolly looked up at the man. "Now," she said in a trembling voice, "so are you!"

Talbot studied her coldly from on high, then he turned and vanished. A moment later, the front door of the ranch house burst open and a half dozen men wearing nothing but their longjohns and their gunbelts shoved their way inside.

"It's Frank Beavers!" a gunman shouted. "It's her damned brother!"

They all looked up at the broken landing rail, then back at Dolly. One of the Rocking T gunfighters snickered, "I guess your poor brother just came to pay you a little social call, huh, Dolly?"

The others laughed but Dolly paid them no mind. Her heart was consumed with grief. Frank had come to save her and she'd distracted him and gotten him killed.

When Dolly heard the front door bang shut, she found her brother's six-gun. Picking it up with a shaking hand, she climbed to her feet.

When the right time comes and I've got what I need, she vowed silently, I'll kill him myself.

NINE

DARBY BUCKINGHAM topped a low, rocky ridge to see Frank Beavers's cabin. Even more important, he saw Hallelujah and Austin's fine palomino penned in the corral. He didn't see the mule but that came as no great surprise.

Darby shifted Austin's weight on his shoulder and continued on to the cabin. He kicked open the sagging door and bulled his way inside. The place was a pigsty, causing Darby to about-face. He carried Austin back outside and laid him on the ground. Darby strode over to a sweating oaken water barrel and found a tin cup. He filled it and returned to Austin's side.

"Here," he said, kneeling next to the still unconscious man, "drink this."

Austin moaned as Darby poured a little water into his mouth. Austin choked and Darby sloshed water onto his young friend's face. He slapped Austin's cheeks a few times, rather roughly, then stood up and hunted for their saddles. He found them lying in some weeds near the corral. Darby also found their bridles and blankets. In less than a quarter of an hour, Hallelujah was ready to ride.

"Austin," he said, returning to the man, "can you hear me?"

Austin's eyelids quivered.

"I need to go to the Rocking T Ranch," Darby said.

"That's where I'll find Frank Beavers, more likely dead than alive by now. Can you ride?"

Austin muttered something and Darby studied the young Easterner's face. "I don't think you're up to it," he said. "And I can't afford to wait. Come along if you can—if not, I'll see you back in Whiskey Creek."

He left Austin in the yard with another cup of water close at hand. Darby decided not to saddle the young man's horse. If Austin was going to come after him, he had to be at least strong enough to saddle that spirited palomino.

Darby wished he had his double-barreled shotgun, but he still had his derringer; if he could find the Rocking T Ranch from earlier directions, then he'd do all right. It was going to seem damned strange facing Dolly under these circumstances, but the meeting had to take place if Darby was ever going to regain his normal peace of mind.

"I just hope that double-crossing Frank Beavers hasn't messed up everything," Darby muttered as he prodded Hallelujah into a shambling trot.

Darby spent a cold and hungry night wrapped up in his horse blanket under the shadow of a boulder. Early the following morning, he warmed his stiff hands over a little fire; then he resaddled Hallelujah and used a fallen log to remount.

"Unless we've strayed off course, it can't be more than another five or ten miles to the Rocking T Ranch," he told the horse.

Hallelujah was in a very nasty mood. His ears were laid back and he'd nipped when Darby pinched his hide in the cinch ring while drawing it up too tightly. Fearing the beast would desert and leave him stranded in the Laramies, Darby had kept the horse tied all night on a short rope to a stout tree. Hallelujah was cranky from hunger and that was fine, because Darby felt exactly the same.

Darby had been following a trail he hoped was Frank's,

and he felt quite confident that he would soon arrive at the perimeter of the Rocking T Ranch. At midmorning his confidence was rewarded when he came upon a few Rocking T branded cattle. They viewed him with suspicion and were as wild-eyed as deer. The Derby Man paid them no mind. He rode Hallelujah around the cattle and kept moving north until a pair of cowboys spotted him and came forward at a high lope. When they drew close enough to see Darby clearly, their faces reflected shock, then amusement.

"Well, what the hell are you!" one of them called, pulling his horse to a sliding stop and gawking at Darby as if he had come from another planet.

"My name is Darby Buckingham. I've come to see Mr. Talbot."

The two cowboys exchanged looks before one said, "You a friend of Mr. Talbot?"

"No," Darby confessed, "but I very much look forward to making his acquaintance."

"What the hell you want with him?"

"That," Darby snapped, "is really none of your business."

The taller of the pair, a lantern-jawed man in his late twenties, turned belligerent. "Mr. Buckingham," he spat, "we're going to *make* it our business."

Darby's hand slipped into his coat pocket and he drew out the two-shot derringer. It was almost completely enveloped in his big fist, except for the barrel, and that was enough to achieve his purpose.

"Why hell, Mr. Buckingham," the silent one stammered, "why don't you just put that thing away! Ain't our job to say who comes and goes on this spread. We're just a couple of cowpunchers. Ain't that right, Art?"

Art was slow to answer, but when Darby shifted the barrel of the mean-looking little weapon in his general direction, he nodded quite energetically. "Sure is!"

"Good," Darby said, "then why don't you cowpunchers

just reach across with your left hands and unholster those sidearms. Then drop them and ride away."

"What!"

"You heard me."

The cowboys weren't happy about that but they did as they were ordered. And after they'd dropped their six-guns, Darby said, "Now ride and don't stop until you're out of my sight."

"You're going to pay for this!" Art swore. "You're on Rocking T range now and you'll answer."

"If I do," Darby said, "it won't be to the likes of you. Is the ranch house straight ahead?"

"About four miles is all," the other man said. "And we'll be along before sundown to take an accounting, mister."

"It will be my pleasure to accommodate you both," Darby said, climbing stiffly down from the saddle and retrieving their six-guns. He shoved them into his coat pockets and then waited as the riders trotted off to disappear over a ridge. They'd angle back and tail him but Darby was certain they'd not try to drop him with their saddle rifles, at least until they had Jim Talbot's permission.

As soon as he saw the ranch headquarters, Darby had to admit that he felt a knot ball up in his gut—not out of fear of Jim Talbot, but rather about meeting Dolly under these distressing circumstances. What was he going to say to her? She was a married woman, and Darby, knowing what he did about Talbot, was not in a mood to be cordial to her long lost rancher husband.

And then there was the question of Frank Beavers. Was he still alive or had he been shot trying to kill Talbot? These were the questions that preyed on his mind.

To hell with it, he told himself, pushing Hallelujah into a hard gallop that brought him bouncing into the ranch-yard. His arrival attracted plenty of attention. Men dropped what they were doing in the barn and the black-smith shop to stare at the dude in the derby who rode so poorly.

The insides of Darby's legs were chafed and on fire. He was hungry, dirty and in no mood to be trifled with. What he wanted—and all he wanted—was a simple explanation from Dolly Beavers as to the reason she'd deceived and then jilted him. After that, he'd go in peace and do his damnedest to put her out of his mind.

"Derby!"

Darby was in the act of dismounting and her voice rattled him so badly that he tried to turn before his left foot was free of the stirrup. The result was totally humiliating and he crashed to the ground. It was then that he saw his Dolly leaning out of an upstairs window.

"Blast!" he roared as the Rocking T cowboys hooted with laughter.

"Oh, Derby!" she cried.

He bounced to his feet, cruel laughter ringing in his ears. "*Darby!*" he shouted up at her in anger. "Will you *never* remember!"

She looked at him for a moment with such joy, and then her lovely face crumpled. Dolly burst into tears and she vanished from his sight.

Darby stared at the open window for a moment. What a strange reaction! He tied Hallelujah to a hitch rail and slapped the dust from his pants, aware of how poor a figure he presented to these ignorant cowboys. He probably looked quite ridiculous to them.

Jim Talbot appeared. He was, Darby had to concede, tall and handsome, well dressed and totally assured. Darby remembered the description given him in Reno of the rancher's eyes and found that they were indeed without a trace of either charity or kindness.

"You're the Derby Man, aren't you?" Talbot said, crossing his arms on his chest and leaning against a porch post.

"That's right." Darby squared his shoulders. "I've come to see Dolly and find out about her brother."

Talbot grinned wickedly. "I shot him to death last night.

In fact, we'll be burying him in a few hours. So if you'd like to attend his planting, be my guest."

Darby's eyes flicked back up to the window. "I want to see Dolly."

"Mrs. Talbot is busy." The grin died on the rancher's lips. "Besides, I don't believe that you were invited to this ranch."

Darby started to say something but he was interrupted by the sight of Dolly climbing out through her window.

"Damn you, Jim Talbot!" she shouted. "How dare you lock me up in my room!"

And then, before Talbot could leap off the porch and see her, Dolly lost her balance and came rolling down the steeply canted porch roof.

Darby jumped forward, and when the woman took sail he was in position to catch her in his strong arms. Dolly opened her eyes, saw who had saved her, squealed with happiness and then planted a kiss on Darby's lips. For just an instant, Darby forgot the situation. For one delicious, delirious moment, he was overcome with pure joy.

Talbot changed all that. He planted his feet in front and delivered a powerful overhand right that caught Darby in the temple and spilled him and Dolly into the dirt. Darby's head spun around and, before he made the spinning stop, the toe of Talbot's boot crashed into his ribs.

Darby knew that at least one of them was cracked. He could hear Dolly screaming as he pushed himself to his hands and knees. Years of fighting had given him a sixth sense of danger and now it came into play. Darby rolled sideways, barely avoiding another vicious kick that would have caught him under the jaw and put him down for keeps.

He staggered to his feet, vaguely aware of Dolly trying to fend off the rancher with her small fists. Talbot batted her aside, and when he lashed out again with his boot, Darby was ready. He caught the man's foot and twisted it savagely. Talbot grunted with pain and fell hard. Darby was on him instantly, fists slamming into the man's face like sledgehammers spiking down rails over railroad ties.

"Get him!" Dolly was screaming. "Derby, beat his brains in!"

Darby wouldn't take things that far but with a cracked rib and all the anger he had inside, he was going to do his level best to permanently rearrange the man's handsome, arrogant face. And he would have, if some cowboy hadn't pistol-whipped him across the back of the head in spite of all that Dolly could do. Darby felt as if he were spinning down the center of a bottomless well filled with darkness and Dolly's hysterical screams. An instant later, his world went silent and black.

When Darby awoke, it was dark outside and he was tied to one of the heavy posts that supported the porch. Dolly was nowhere to be seen but there were plenty of cowboys gathered around, watching.

"He's awake," one of them said. "Better go get the boss."

A few minutes later, Jim Talbot appeared. In contrast to his first impression, Darby now witnessed an entirely different man. This one wasn't as handsome because his face was bruised and one eye was swollen shut. He wasn't smiling, probably because his lips were broken and they'd have bled if he tried. Darby shook his head and thought that his brains had been replaced by broken bottles. The pain was instant, cutting him to the core.

"Too bad you didn't just let me see Dolly," he growled. "It appears that it would have been a lot easier on both of us."

Someone dragged over a cane-bottomed rocking chair for the rancher and he sat down heavily. "I should kill you right now. I could do it fast—or slow. Either way, it would give me great satisfaction."

"How much satisfaction do you need?" Darby asked. "You've already killed Frank Beavers. Isn't one man enough this week?"

Talbot leaned forward and his hands were balled into fists. "Is that supposed to be funny?"

"I want to see Dolly. And I want to see her alone."

Talbot scoffed. "I'll give you this much, you've got some nerve riding in here and demanding to see my wife alone." He looked around at his cowboys and gunfighters. "Doesn't this man have some nerve, boys!"

They all nodded and murmured that Darby did, indeed, have nerve.

"Boys," Talbot said, leaning back in his rocking chair and cocking one leg over the other, "did you hear what this dude said? He said he wants to see my wife—alone! Now, if that ain't grounds for killin' a man for taking improper liberties, then I don't know what is."

The crew noisily agreed.

"Where's Dolly?" Darby asked. "Locked in her room again? How are you keeping her from jumping back out of the window? Did you shackle her to the bed?"

"No, but that's not a bad idea," Talbot said with a lascivious wink that made Darby's blood boil. "A woman built like Dolly *ought* to be chained to a man's bed."

It was all Darby could do to keep quiet.

Talbot watched him closely. "Dolly and I just had another long talk about you. And honest to Pete, I'm just not sure what I'm going to do with you, Mr. Derby Man. You're famous enough to cause a big stir if you were found someplace either beat to death or shot."

"Then let me go."

"I could do that, providing you'd give me your word never to come back. Dolly tells me you are a man of your word. Is she right?"

"She is."

"Then I could do that," Talbot repeated. "But would you go without seeing her first?"

"Never."

"That's what I'm beginning to understand," Talbot said. "So what are you going to do?"

"I don't rightly know just yet," the rancher admitted as he came to his feet. "But I do believe I'll post a guard and sleep on the question. Things always seem clearer in the morning. You ever notice that it works that way, Mr. Derby Man?"

Darby chose not to dignify the question with an answer.

Talbot turned to his men. "I want two gunnies guarding this man all night. Cowboys, get to bed. Despite all the excitement, this is still a cattle ranch."

The Rocking T gunfighters held a little powwow and two of them stayed while the others trailed after the cowboys toward the bunkhouse.

Talbot watched them go, then turned to say to Darby, "I suppose you're hungry and thirsty?"

Darby swallowed his pride. He was so hungry he felt weak and he had a raging thirst.

"I'll send something out in a few minutes. Might be your last supper, so enjoy it."

Darby just glared at the cattleman, but a few minutes later when Dolly rushed out onto the porch with a big tray of food and drink, he was very grateful.

"Git!" Dolly shouted at the gunmen. "Git away from us!"

"We're guarding him!"

"Then do it from a distance. This man isn't going anywhere."

The gunmen surprised Darby by walking off a short distance. He looked up at Dolly and saw that her eyes were swollen from crying. "You must have some influence around here, Dolly. They wouldn't have minded me worth a damn if I'd ordered them to move off a ways."

"Ohh . . . shhh!" Dolly picked up a glass of brandy and stooped to pour some down Darby's parched throat. "With your hands tied, I'm afraid this eating and drinking business is going to be a little messy."

The brandy burned all the way down. "I'd rather have water," he croaked.

She started to rise and go back inside but Darby said, "Never mind. Give me some more and then the food."

Dolly, with her heart-shaped face, gold ringlets and sensuous lips, was still a vision of loveliness to Darby, but he could see that she'd changed. He no longer saw the joy that normally made her big blue eyes sparkle.

"Why did you come here?" he asked.

"We buried my brother today," she said. "I know he also wondered why I returned after so many years."

"And you never told him?"

"Here," Dolly said, holding a chicken leg up for Darby to gnaw.

He ripped the meat from the leg and swallowed it greedily. "Tell me, Dolly, why did you come back! Was it to get a divorce? Because, if it was, I could have hired the finest lawyers and we'd have gotten a divorce, if not an outright annulment. And even if that were impossible, then . . ."

She placed the palm of her hand across his greasy lips. "Darby, honey, love. That's only part of it. I . . ." Dolly could not quite bring up the words.

"What!"

When she could finally speak, she said, "I gave him my babies!"

Darby stopped chewing. "Babies?"

"Yes. They were twins. A boy and a girl. He made me give them up and I've never seen them since. Their names are . . . Jim and . . ."

"Tracy."

She stared. "How did you know that! Did he tell you?"

"I learned about them when I returned to Reno, only I didn't understand then," Darby said, remembering the names he'd first heard in Reno. No wonder Jim Tracy had been such a mysterious and elusive character. He didn't exist.

Dolly sniffled. "I *have* to see them again! And he promised that I would if I returned. I thought I could also get a divorce and then come back to find you with a clear conscience. I never thought that it would work out like this."

"So," Darby said, "we're both caught in Talbot's web."

Dolly nodded.

"What can I do?" Darby asked, wishing with all his heart that he could comfort Dolly in the shelter of his arms.

"I want you to go away and leave me," she said in a flat but determined voice.

"Not if you want to come with me."

"I want to more than life, but . . ."

"Then we'll go together and we'll find those children. Give me another drumstick, please."

"Oh, sure. Sorry."

Darby devoured the meat. "Any idea where your twins are now?"

"No." Dolly looked over her shoulder, then leaned close and whispered. "I've even searched through his files and desk, hoping I'd find some clue. But there's nothing!"

"If I live past tomorrow morning," Darby vowed, "I'll help you find them, no matter how long it takes."

"Then you don't hate me?"

"Of course not. I think you're very . . . could I have that piece of . . . what is it?"

"Roast beef. Just the way you like it," she said, stabbing a forkful and feeding it to him.

"Oh, excellent!" he said, smacking his lips.

"What were you going to say a moment ago?"

"About what?"

"You know. About me being very . . ."

"Oh. Yes. I just think that it was a little foolish of you not to have joined me at Promontory Point to explain this situation. It would have been so much easier on both of us."

"But you don't understand. I *was* coming to join you until the very moment that Jim showed up at the hotel in Reno. And after he told me about my children, well, I just lost my senses."

She forked more roast beef into his mouth. "I hope you

can find it in your heart to forgive me. This all happened when I was so young. I couldn't stay and he wouldn't let me take the babies, so I ran."

"How did the man find you after all these years?"

"He saw a newspaper article telling that our wedding would take place when the rails were joined. It said that I was staying in Reno and would be going to meet you the moment the transcontinental railroad was completed. He didn't have to look very hard when he came to Nevada."

"I see." Darby chewed his food thoughtfully. "More brandy, if you please."

"Of course."

"I'm sorry about your brother."

At the mention of her brother, Dolly burst into fresh tears; this was very hard on Darby because all he could do was eat and watch the dear woman suffer. But tomorrow morning, God and Jim Talbot willing, he'd be set free and then he'd find a way to save Dolly from this monster and make everything right.

"Umm . . . ah, Dolly darling?"

She looked up.

"Did you bake those biscuits?"

"Uh-huh."

"Would you spread a little of that jelly on them for me? Is it grape or . . ."

"Crabapple."

"Sounds delicious," Darby said, forcing a brave smile.

"I just love to watch you eat," Dolly cooed. "It makes you such a big strong man."

Darby smiled. "I don't suppose you brought a knife along with that fork, did you?"

Dolly shook her head and pouted. "He made sure that I did not."

The Derby Man leaned back very hard against the post and felt it quiver. "Maybe I won't need one anyway."

"But what can I do to help?"

"If you hear the front porch crash down in the middle of the night, come running."

Dolly's eyes widened with alarm. "But you could be crushed to death!"

"Hmmm. You may be right." Darby scowled. "What do you think the chances are that Talbot will turn me loose tomorrow morning?"

"You can never predict what he'll do."

Darby's mind raced. "If I'm not free by two o'clock this morning, sneak down with a gun and a knife and we'll do the best that we can."

"But he'll lock me in my room!"

"There's another way down," Darby said, knowing she wasn't going to like his suggestion. "You could always climb out the window again."

"But you won't be able to catch me!"

"Then never mind," Darby said. "Just do the best you can and . . . is that pumpkin pie?"

"Your favorite."

"Hmmm!" Darby said, and opened his mouth wide.

TEN

AUSTIN APPLEGATE'S HEAD still felt as if it had been split by a meat cleaver. Every bounce of his seat against the saddle caused waves of pain to radiate up and down his spine. Even his teeth ached. Despite all this he rode with a fixed purpose, knowing that Darby Buckingham was going to need his assistance.

It had been almost evening when he'd taken to the trail; but although darkness came quickly in the Laramie Mountains, making it very difficult to follow a trail, the palomino he rode was a Rocking T Ranch horse and it had the instincts of a homing pigeon. Austin simply dropped his reins and let the animal pick the most direct trail through the high mountains. All that was required was to hold on to his saddlehorn and try not to lose consciousness, and this, Austin was able to do. Morning found him moving steadily on the Rocking T range with the palomino covering ground as methodically as a machine.

Once he thought he'd seen a low trail of dust on the northern horizon and he'd pulled into a stand of pines. A quarter of an hour later, Austin was glad he'd taken the precaution because he saw a pair of Rocking T riders galloping at a cross-angle, also heading north.

Austin waited until they were well out of sight, and then he moved out of the trees. Dammit, he raged to himself, all he carried was a nearly useless little pearl-handled derringer! How was that supposed to be of any value against a bunch of gunfighters? Austin did not know the answer to his question but he did know that he could not live with himself if he didn't at least try to help Darby Buckingham.

Early afternoon found him within sight of the distant ranch headquarters. The high-spirited palomino was so eager to reach a stall with hay and grain that it bent its head low, opened its mouth wide, and ran toward the ranchyard.

"Whoa! Damn you, whoa!"

But the powerful animal was far stronger than Austin. Head down, red nostrils flared, it ran as hard as it could. Austin cussed and stood up in his stirrups, hauling on the reins until one of them broke.

"Blast!" he shouted in frustration, seeing cowboys leap to their horses and gallop forward to intercept him. Austin gave the horse its head and held on for his life.

The palomino shot right through the crowd of onrushing riders, passing through them like a hot blade slicing butter, and didn't stop running until it planted its feet in front of the hitching rail by the ranch house.

Austin was so busy hanging on that it wasn't until he stopped that he saw Darby Buckingham lashed to a porch post. Behind him stood a man who could only be Jim Talbot.

"Hello, Mr. Applegate," Darby said in a surprisingly cheerful tone of voice, considering his position. "How good of you to return that fine animal to Mr. Talbot."

"What's going on here?" Talbot demanded, charging around the hitch rail to drag Austin from his saddle. "This is my gelding. I traded him off in Reno! What—"

"Well, sir," Austin said with enormous aplomb, "I just thought he was probably homesick and so I brought him back."

Darby grinned. If he and Austin survived, he was going to do everything possible to see that the young man became a successful dime novelist. He certainly had flair and the ability to handle pressure.

Talbot swung around to face Darby. He saw Dolly now, standing beside the Derby Man, and that made him even angrier. "Darby, who is this young fool?"

"He's my . . . protégé," Darby announced.

"A writer?"

Darby ignored the contempt in the rancher's voice. "That is correct."

"I have trespassers shot!"

"Can I quote you on that, Mr. Talbot?" Austin asked with such pure innocence that Darby wanted to clap his hands.

"Quote me?" Talbot balled his fists. "What I'm going to do is . . ."

"If you kill him," Darby said, "you'll have federal marshals all over this place. Mr. Applegate's father is a rich and influential fellow. He'd hire the Pinkertons."

"The Pinkertons?"

"That's right," Darby said. "I'm sure you've heard of that esteemed investigative agency."

"I thought they worked for the railroads and stage lines."

"They work for anyone who pays them," Austin said. "And my father pays very well."

Jim Talbot turned away and everyone heard him curse. He began to stride back and forth across the porch, his boots banging on the boards.

"What am I to do with you?" he said, stopping and looking directly at Darby.

"Let me go. What harm can I or Mr. Applegate cause you now?"

"You want Dolly."

"She's your wife."

"She wants a divorce."

"Then give it to her! Slavery has been abolished, in case you haven't heard."

"Never!" Talbot shouted angrily.

Darby glanced at Dolly. He saw the tears well up in her eyes. "Why don't we fight for her?"

"Ha! She's told me that you were a bareknuckles champion. I'm not about to do that. We could, however, face each other with six-guns."

"Darby, no!" Dolly pleaded.

Darby ignored her. "That is your choice."

"It'd be a fair fight," Talbot said. "The one that is left standing keeps Dolly."

"I won't be a party to this murder!" Dolly cried. "Jim, if you do this, I'll find a way to kill you in your sleep. I swear that I will!"

Talbot's shoulders slumped. "Well then," he said, "I don't see much point in a gunfight, even one I couldn't possibly lose."

"Let me go," Darby said.

"And you'll really go? You and your writer friend?"

"We will. But first I must talk to Dolly alone."

Talbot turned to Dolly. "Right now—tell everyone I killed your brother in self-defense."

Dolly's blue eyes misted. "That's the truth."

"Did everyone just hear her?" Talbot demanded. "I had a right to kill her brother."

"Then you've committed no crime save keeping me tied to this porch post," Darby snapped. "So untie me!"

Talbot dipped his chin once, but quite emphatically. "All right," he said, pulling out a pocket knife and cutting the ropes that bound Darby.

Darby stood up very unsteadily. He rubbed his wrists to restore their circulation and said, "Now leave Dolly and me alone for a few minutes."

"I don't think I want to do that," Talbot decided. "What you have to say to my wife, you can also say to me."

Darby took a deep breath; then his neck sank into his massive round shoulders a little and he suddenly whipped his right fist upward, catching Jim Talbot just under the point of his chin. The big man's head snapped back and he was lifted completely off the ground. Before he landed, Darby snatched his six-gun from its holster and placed its barrel against Talbot's head.

"Shoot me and he's a dead man!" Darby cried out to the nearby gunmen as he cocked back the hammer.

There were some very fast gunmen in the crowd but the Derby Man's action had taken them completely by surprise. Even Austin was dumbfounded. "What the . . ."

Darby ignored his young friend. "I'm going to have my private talk with Dolly before I leave. So everyone get back out into the yard and we'll all live to see another day. Try to shoot me and your paycheck is gone."

Dolly threw her arms around Darby's neck and hugged him tightly. "Here," Darby choked, handing the gun to Austin, "you keep it trained on Talbot while I step away and have a word with Dolly."

The Derby Man had to actually pry himself away from Dolly and then take her hands into his own and lead her off to the side. There was a pair of rocking chairs at the end of the porch and Darby sat down in one, indicating she should sit in the other.

"Sit," he ordered in a gentle voice.

"Are you really going to leave me?"

"I have to—but I'll be back soon. Dolly, I'm going to find those children and the best Wyoming lawyer money can buy. We're going to cut Jim Talbot right out of your life. But to do that, I have to leave you behind and take care of business."

"But why can't I go?"

Darby said with firmness, "There's about thirty reasons standing right out in the yard. At least six of them are professional gunfighters. They'd never let us get out of here alive. We'd all be shot down. What's the point in dying, when in a few short weeks I can return with a marshal and a court summons—and maybe even your long lost children?"

Dolly covered her face with her hands and wept.

"Get ahold of yourself," Darby urged. "I know how much you want to come with me. But surely you can see how fatal that course of action would be."

"Yes," she said, sniffling. "And Mr. Applegate is so young and gallant. So tall and handsome. Where *did* you find him?"

Darby's mustache twitched. "It's not important. The main thing is, we will find your children and a lawyer who will see that your marriage is dissolved."

Dolly managed to nod her head. "But how will you even begin to . . ."

"There are ways," he said, though none came immediately to his mind. "Someone must know where they were sent or what became of them. Do you have anyone in mind who might help solve this mystery?"

Dolly thought a moment. "Yes, there is," she said. "My childhood friend, Ginger. She might know where they've gone."

Darby sighed and shook his head. "I'm afraid that Ginger is gone. Austin, in a fit of extreme generosity, gave the woman enough money to escape and start her life over."

"What a wonderful thing to do!"

"Yes, but that does rather complicate things for us, doesn't it?" He frowned. "Why do you think that this woman might know what happened to your children?"

"Because," Dolly said, "for the first year or so after I left, I believe she cared for them as if they were her very own."

"What!"

"You have to understand that the woman was in love with Jim, and after I left he used her to care for the twins. She stayed until it became obvious that Jim would never obtain a legal divorce from me to marry her."

"And then she abandoned them?"

"No. It's my understanding that Ginger finally gave Jim an ultimatum and he drove her out. It wasn't long after that that he sent the children away."

"With whom?"

"I don't know. Knowing Jim, he probably hired some poor couple in Whiskey Creek to take them far away, possibly to put in an orphanage or maybe to raise themselves."

"But no one knows anything about this?"

"If Ginger does, she might not tell for fear of her life."

"Did the woman have any close friends?"

"I don't know," Dolly said. "I tried several times to have her bring the children to Running Springs. But my letters and pleas went unanswered. Until the night when Jim and I stayed in Whiskey Creek, I had not laid eyes on the poor woman in almost twenty years."

Darby sighed. "I may have to send Austin back to Reno to track the woman down. But hopefully that won't be necessary. Bribery is very effective. I'll pay handsomely to get the clue we need. And in the meantime, I'll hire that lawyer."

"No one in Cheyenne would dare oppose Jim," Dolly said. "They know that he's violent and treacherous enough to have them killed."

"Then I'll go to Denver."

Dolly nodded. She swallowed and dried her eyes. "I never let Jim touch me," she whispered. "I told him I loved you and I'd kill him if he forced his attentions on me."

"I knew that," Darby said. "And if I didn't know that we'd die if I'd broken his neck just now, he'd be dead and we'd be on our way out of this mess."

"You'd better go before he comes to or he'll kill you and the consequences be damned," Dolly said. "But first, I could pack you and Mr. Applegate a few sandwiches and . . ."

"There's no time. But if you have a pie or something, it would be much appreciated."

"There's one I baked fresh, it's in the pantry. I'll get it and a few other things and be right back."

She returned in minutes with a sack filled with the pie

and also cookies, candy and several loaves of fresh sourdough bread.

"They're warm," he said.

"Right out of the oven," Dolly said, "just the way you like it."

Darby took the sack, then kissed Dolly goodbye before he beckoned to Austin. "This is Dolly," he said, by way of introduction.

"Honored," Austin said with a nervous smile and the six-gun still pointed out toward the gunfighters. "Mr. Buckingham, how are we going to do this?"

Darby took his gun and handed it to Dolly. In a voice loud enough to be heard by everyone, he said, "Dolly, point this at Mr. Talbot. If anyone moves before we are out of range, shoot him!"

Dolly held the gun.

"Listen up," Darby said. "If anyone tries to interfere with our leaving, Miss Beavers will shoot your boss. Is that clear?"

"In a pig's eye, she would," a tall man with a tie-down gun snarled.

"In a pig's eye, I wouldn't!" Dolly shouted, marching to stand over the prostrate form of the rancher.

A long silence was broken when Austin whispered, "Let's get out of here—now!"

Darby was in complete agreement. He dared not turn around and look at Dolly for he knew he might well have a change of heart and foolishly decide to try and get her away now.

"Bring our horses!" Darby shouted at the Rocking T cowboys.

Hallelujah was brought out a few minutes later, and Darby prepared to mount him. Austin had other plans, however. Ignoring the barn-sour palomino, he chose a long-legged roan with an intelligent look to its eyes. A cowboy was holding onto its reins.

"Hey! That's my favorite!" the cowboy howled as Austin snatched the reins from his fist.

"*Was* your favorite," Austin corrected, vaulting into the saddle and waiting anxiously until the Derby Man struggled onto his horse.

"Let's ride!" Austin said anxiously.

Darby needed no urging. He could not help but glance back at Dolly who made him enormously proud by blowing him a kiss.

The Derby Man tipped his battered derby hat to the fair lady, then kicked his horse into a fast trot and went bouncing off toward Whiskey Creek.

ELEVEN

"YOU KNOW," Darby said, licking up the last crumbs of the cherry pie as they rode toward Whiskey Creek, "leaving that woman was the hardest thing I've ever had to do."

"But it was the only intelligent option," Austin said. "We wouldn't have gotten into the saddle before we'd been riddled by those gunfighters. You had no choice, Mr. Buckingham."

"True, but that doesn't seem to be much consolation."

"So what are we going to do now?"

"We're going to canvass Whiskey Creek and try to find out if anyone knows the whereabouts of Dolly's children."

Austin looked skeptical. "Do you really think anyone would tell us, even if they did know?"

"Probably not," Darby admitted. "But a healthy bribe has been known to loosen the lips."

"How much will you offer?"

Without hesitation, Darby said, "I'll offer whatever it takes."

When they arrived back at Whiskey Creek, Darby and Austin checked into their rooms, then immediately headed back out onto the street. They each took a side, walking from establishment to establishment, talking to anyone who'd listen.

"Did you know that Jim Talbot had two children?" Darby would ask, always receiving either a blank stare or a negative reply. He would add, "I'll pay handsomely for information as to their whereabouts."

"How much?" most asked, out of curiosity.

"Plenty," was the Derby Man's curt answer.

Given the small population of the little rail town, it took only a few hours before everyone in Whiskey Creek knew about the two children and the fact that there was a rather large reward being offered.

"All we can do now," Darby said as they settled into easy chairs in his hotel room, "is sit back and wait to see what happens."

"And if nothing does?"

Darby lit a Cuban, sipped his brandy and blew a smoke ring at the ceiling. He was tired, depressed and very impatient. Just the idea of Dolly being stuck at the Rocking T Ranch with that despot, Jim Talbot, was almost more than he could stand.

"Mr. Buckingham?"

He roused himself from his somber reflections. "Mr. Applegate, if we don't hear anything by the time the next westbound train arrives on its way to Reno, then I want you to go there and find Miss Ginger. Dolly said that the woman is our best hope for information."

"Very well." Austin frowned. "I imagine that Miss . . . what was her name?"

"Puddingstone. Miss Dora Puddingstone," Darby said, feeling his cheeks warm a little at the memory of her predatory behavior at the train depot.

"Yes! I'll have to write that down," Austin said, taking a pad and pencil from his pocket and making an entry.

Two days later when the westbound train arrived, Darby still had not received any information about Dolly's children.

"Mr. Applegate, I see no alternative but for you to travel to Reno and try to find the woman that Dolly says took care of her children."

"Even if I find Miss Puddingstone," Austin said as they

stood on the platform, "there's no guarantee that she'll talk."

"Given what you did to help her, I think she will," Darby said. "She must have some sort of loyalty to the children and to Dolly. And now that she's beyond the grasp of Jim Talbot, I can't see what would prevent her from telling you where we can find those children."

"I hope you're right. But I regret leaving you here."

"I won't stay. I'm going to hire a carriage to take me to Cheyenne tomorrow where I'll inquire about an attorney. If none dares oppose Jim Talbot, I'll continue on to Denver."

Austin was silent for a moment. "How will I know where to reach you if I find out something important?"

"Good question." Darby considered it a moment. "Send identical telegrams, one here, one to Cheyenne and one to Denver. I'm bound to be in one of those places."

A few minutes later Austin boarded the train, and as it pulled out of the station Darby realized he was going to miss the young man. He trudged heavily back toward the hotel, but finding the prospect of sitting alone in his room rather depressing, he changed his mind and angled toward Bert, whose boots were hooked over a rail outside the saloon and whose battered Stetson was pulled down over his face. When Darby took the chair next to the stove-up old broncbuster, his dog roused itself enough to thump its tail on the boardwalk a few times.

"How are you doing today, Bert?" Darby asked.

The old man thumbed his hat back and turned his cloudy eyes toward Darby. He squinted and said, "That you, Derby Man?"

"It is. Want a beer?"

"If you're buyin', I damn sure do!"

"I'm buying," Darby said, grateful for a little company, even if the old cowhand would gulp his drinks like a man dying of thirst.

"I'd like it even better if you was to buy whiskey instead of beer."

"Beer," Darby said, knowing that Bert had a reputation for getting belligerent on hard liquor.

"Dog wouldn't mind a pickled egg or two," Bert added.

"Fine," Darby said, heading into the saloon with Bert and his mangy red dog shuffling along behind.

"Beers," Darby said to O'Brien.

The Irishman nodded. There wasn't another customer in the place and Darby thought the man looked pretty forlorn. "Why don't *you* have one on me, O'Brien."

"Well thank you!" the bartender said. "And to your good health, Mr. Buckingham!"

"And also to yours," Darby said, raising his frothy glass.

Bert gulped his beer and slammed his glass down. " 'Nother would be fine," he announced hopefully.

O'Brien looked at Darby who nodded and said, "Keep them coming all around."

That suited the bartender just fine. He downed his own beer in a few gulps and Darby did the same. During the next hour, they each drank half a dozen glasses of beer and all three of them were feeling a whole lot better about life.

"Yes, sir," Bert was saying, "when I was breaking mustangs for the Rocking T, we had some wild times, for certain."

"How long ago would that be—fifty years or so?" O'Brien asked, winking at Darby.

"Fifty years, my foot! Ten is about right."

O'Brien hooted. "You haven't swung a leg over a horse in a good fifteen years!"

Bert puffed up like a blowfish. "Why, the hell I haven't! I was busting broncs when I was fifty years old! That was just five years ago!"

O'Brien laughed out loud and Bert got so angry he tossed his beer into the bartender's face. O'Brien's fist shot out and he grabbed Bert by the collar and was about to pull him off his feet when Darby's hand clamped down on his wrist. "Why don't we keep it friendly, O'Brien."

The Irishman winced with pain at Darby's vise-like grip.

"Sure," he grunted, pulling back until Darby released him. "I just get tired of hearing that old blowhard go on and on about how great he was breaking horses."

"Why, you no-account . . ."

"Hey!" Darby said. "If you two don't behave, I'm going to stop buying beer and walk out of here, leaving you to kill each other."

O'Brien managed a weak laugh. "All right," he said, "I was just trying to have a few laughs. It ain't easy to find something to laugh about in Whiskey Creek."

"Well, don't laugh at your customer's expense," Darby warned. "You ought to know better."

"Yeah, you Irish idiot!" Bert taunted. "I'm a customer!"

"You're an old drunken cowboy is what you are," O'Brien said. "And you're a windbag to boot!"

The two men lunged for each other and Darby had to separate them. If he had not been so desperate for company, he'd have let them kill each other and good riddance.

"Come on," Darby said, grabbing the old man by the belt and propelling him back outside to his chair on the boardwalk. "Sit down and behave yourself."

Bert wasn't happy. "What are we doing out here if all the beer is inside!" he said, jerking his thumb over his shoulder toward O'Brien's saloon.

"Behave yourself and I'll get us a bottle and a couple of glasses."

"You will?"

"That's right. But I'll pour and you'll slow down a little."

"Good enough," Bert said, totally mollified. "Whatever you say, since you're the man that's buying."

Darby left the man and went back into the saloon. O'Brien was angry and drinking a little whiskey to calm himself.

"That old fool has got to die one of these days," he groused. "Be a blessing for everyone in Whiskey Creek when he passes on."

"Give me a bottle of your best whiskey," Darby said.

"If you're going to let him have most of it, you might as well buy rotgut for half the price," O'Brien muttered. "That blind old goat won't know the difference anyway."

"Rotgut is not my style," Darby said curtly, "and you are ill-suited to be a bartender."

O'Brien's cheeks reddened and he started to sass Darby, but when he looked into the man's black eyes he changed his mind.

"Be two dollars," he snapped. "Best whiskey I've got."

Darby paid the man for the whiskey and the beer and went outside. Evening was falling across the land and some low clouds off to the east were colored crimson and gold. Darby sat down with the bottle and two glasses. He filled them both and handed one to Bert.

"To better days," he grunted, raising his glass.

They tossed their whiskey down and Darby watched the brilliant sunset. His slightly fogged mind ranged out to the Rocking T Ranch and he wondered how Dolly was getting along. If Talbot in any way compromised Dolly, Darby would tear the prominent Wyoming rancher limb from limb.

"For a man with money, you don't look very damned happy," Bert commented. "And, furthermore, you are damned slow to pour the whiskey."

Darby roused himself from his ominous thoughts and poured. "I was thinking about Dolly and Talbot and those children," he said. "It's a shame that Dolly might never know her own flesh and blood."

Bert tossed down his drink. Through his cloudy eyes there now gleamed a flame. His voice took on timbre. "You know, them kids might not be worth finding. You ever think of that?"

"What is that supposed to mean?" Darby asked, startled

and then troubled by a possibility that he had not even considered.

"Well, just that they might have turned out wrong and be more bother than they're worth."

"That's possible," Darby conceded, "but it would be nice to find out."

"I hear," Bert said, reaching for the bottle which Darby moved away, "that you're offering quite a pile of cash for information as to where them kids are living."

"That's right." Darby looked at the old man. "If you were working for Talbot then, maybe you saw them when they were sent away."

"Maybe I did. Whiskey has always improved my memory."

Darby poured another drink for them both.

"Yes sir, whiskey and money can do wonders for a poor man's memory," Bert said with a smile on his cracked lips.

Darby reached into his pocket. "I'm carrying about a hundred dollars in my wallet."

"Ain't enough," Bert sighed. "Too risky for pocket money."

"And there's about a hundred more in my coat pocket."

"Still ain't enough."

"And," Darby said, "if I was to actually find Dolly's missing children, I'd be willing to pay even more."

"How much?"

"Another hundred."

Bert glanced back over his shoulder. "Why don't we just say that you'd pay . . . oh . . . five hundred dollars altogether."

Darby raised a thick, bushy eyebrow. "Whiskey talking for you, Bert?"

"Some, maybe. But there's fuel for the fire, if you know what I mean."

"What exactly do you mean?"

"I mean that I have a pretty good hunch where you can find Dolly's kids."

"I'm listening."

Bert leaned close. "If we ride out of Whiskey Creek tonight, it'd take us about a week."

"You'd want to come along?"

"Sure!"

"I don't know. No offense, but you don't look spry enough for a long ride."

"Spry or not, I can outlast you on a horse. But I am worried about my dog, Jake."

Darby could understand that. Old Jake was in pretty bad shape, mangy, half-blind and arthritic, like his master.

"We could ride to the next town and I could rent a carriage," Darby suggested. "We could put Jake in with us and go on."

"And what about whiskey? Would you be willing to stock the carriage with whiskey? Gets mighty cold on the trail at night."

"I would bring some liquor," Darby said. "But first, I'd want to know for certain that I wasn't being tricked."

Bert dipped his pointed chin. "How would you decide?"

"I'd listen to what you said and then make up my mind. What do you really know, Bert?"

"I was there when they came for the children."

"They?"

"That's right."

"Who . . ."

"If I told you, I'd be a complete fool."

"I need more," Darby said.

Bert licked his lips. "All right. It was a man and a woman. They come for the children and I overheard that they were from an orphanage."

"An orphanage!" Darby was shocked. "Why would a man send his own children to an orphanage?"

"Because Jim Talbot was crazy with rage over Dolly leaving. Because he didn't have anywhere else to send them when Ginger went packing back to this town."

"Where was this orphanage?"

"Far away." Bert reached for the bottle, and this time Darby did not try to stop him from pouring his own. "Far, far away, Mr. Derby Man."

Darby let the man drink while he considered what he'd just heard. He wasn't at all sure that he could believe this old drunkard but what other lead did he have? None.

"That's enough," Darby said, taking the bottle away. "If we're riding out tonight, you've got to be sober."

"Sober?" Bert coughed a laugh. "If I'm drunk I ride even better. Always did. Besides, it don't hurt to lubricate the joints."

"They're lubricated enough," Darby said.

"What about that hundred dollars?"

Darby knew better than to give the man that much money now. If he did, Bert would get drunk and stay that way for a month.

"We ride and we find the children first, then you get it all."

"That ain't what we first talked about!"

"Maybe not," Darby said, pushing himself to his feet and pouring the remainder of the whiskey into the street. "But it's my way or no way. Your choice."

Bert stared at the whiskey with longing in his cloudy eyes. "All right," he rasped, "meet me and Jake at the east end of town just after midnight."

Darby nodded his head and then he walked away. At best, he judged it a fifty-fifty proposition that Bert would even show. But since Darby had nothing better to do, he would take the gamble.

At least, now there was hope.

TWELVE

"SAY, HEY?"

Darby stepped out of the shadows, leading Hallelujah. It was so dark that he could barely see the form of the man and his horse. "Bert?"

"Who else would be a'horseback at this hour?"

"What are you carrying?"

"It's Jake," Bert said, riding in closer so that Darby could see the dog wedged between the old broncbuster and the fork of his saddle.

Jake slapped his tail up and down and Darby allowed himself a tight smile. "He looks comfortable enough to travel."

"He is! But the old cuss is puttin' on too much weight," Bert complained. "Had a hell of a time liftin' him into the saddle. And all them pickled eggs he craves give him terrible gas."

"Then I'll keep upwind of you whenever I can," Darby said. "Which way do we ride?"

"East." Without further comment, Bert spurred his rangy but quite handsome buckskin past Darby and lined out, following a road that paralleled the Union Pacific rails.

"This orphanage in Cheyenne?"

"Nope."

Darby pounded Hallelujah's ribs with the heels of his

shoes until the lazy beast caught up with the old man and his dog. "How long will we ride?"

"All night." Bert glanced sideways at him. There was little doubt he could hear the clinking of the four bottles of whiskey Darby had crammed into his saddlebags. "The air has a pretty good nip to 'er. So, how about a little whiskey?"

"Later."

Bert jerked up on his reins so hard that the buckskin practically squatted on its hindquarters.

"No whiskey, no deal." And then, before Darby could even yank his own horse up short, the old man reined his cowpony about smartly and headed back toward Whiskey Creek.

"Hey, wait!" Darby shouted. "All right. You win!"

Bert pulled his horse up, spun it around on its hindlegs and came trotting past with his hand out. Darby slapped a bottle into his fist and the man kept trotting on, forcing Darby to push Hallelujah into a punishing trot.

They trotted for hours until Darby knew that he could stand no more of it. "Hold up!" he called. "We're going to walk the rest of the way."

Bert kept trotting.

"If you won't slow down for my sake, at least slow down for Jake's! I can hear him grunting and passing wind. Have mercy on us!"

The plea worked. Bert slowed to a walk and Darby caught up with the man and glared at him with ill-concealed malevolence. "You sure are stubborn and hard-headed."

"At least I can ride a horse without looking like a sack of beans."

"Where are we going?"

"To Cheyenne."

"Then you lied to me!"

"I lie a lot," Bert confessed.

Darby reached out to grab the man but Jake snapped

viciously at his outstretched hand. Darby yanked his hand back. In the faint starlight, he could see the dog's fangs bared.

"If you're lying about that orphanage," Darby said, "a time of reckoning will soon be at hand."

"I ain't lyin' about that," Bert said. "I'm doin' this for the money—remember? I expect two hundred and fifty dollars when we get to the orphanage and the rest when we find them children."

"You'll get it."

Bert took a long pull on the bottle and, to Darby's amazement, slipped a pickled egg from his coat pocket and gave it to Jake, who wolfed it down. The old dog thumped his tail against the saddle and burped with contentment.

"I don't understand you at all," Darby confessed.

"Ain't important that you do," Bert said, finishing off the bottle and tossing it over his shoulder. He held out his hand. "Just keep me in whiskey. That's all that I need."

Darby reluctantly handed the man another bottle. "If you get too drunk, you'll fall off that horse and break your neck."

"Not a bad way to go," Bert said, uncorking the bottle and taking a long pull. "A lot of worse ways for a broncbuster to cash in his chips."

"I have to find Dolly's children," Darby growled. "After that, you and that vile dog can do whatever you want."

"I'm going to Texas," Bert announced. "Always wanted to see the Alamo where David Crockett and Jim Bowie made their stand. And after that, I think I'll ride down to Old Mexico and cultivate a taste for tequila and frijoles. I've suffered through my last freezin' Wyomin' winter. With five hundred dollars, a man can live out the rest of his days like a king in Old Mexico."

"You keep drinking like you are now," Darby warned, "and your days will be numbered."

Bert turned his cloudy and now bloodshot eyes on the Derby Man. "If you was in my condition," he said, pronouncing his words very distinctly, "you wouldn't give a damn, either."

Darby didn't have anything to say about that, so the three of them rode down out of the Laramie Mountains in a silence that was punctuated frequently by Jake's intestinal problem. At sunrise, they saw the railroad town of Cheyenne with its new roundhouses and trainyard.

"Are you sober enough to remember the name of the orphanage?" Darby asked with irritation.

"It ain't in Cheyenne."

"What the . . ."

"I only said we was *goin'* to Cheyenne." Bert was swaying visibly in the saddle and his face appeared very old and colorless in the early morning light. He looked awful. "We're on our way to Denver."

"Maybe you should just tell me the name of the orphanage in Denver and I can . . ."

"Who said anything about the orphanage *being* in Denver?"

Darby's patience was being severely tried. He would have grabbed the man by the neck and shaken the truth out of him on the spot, except that Jake was watching him with one eye and an exposed and nasty-looking fang.

When they reached Cheyenne, they found a cafe and ordered a big breakfast, despite Bert's protests.

"Instead of more whiskey, you need food and plenty of black coffee," Darby told the man. "And that's all you're getting from me."

Bert was very unhappy but he put away a huge stack of pancakes and half a pound of ham. Jake and Darby had the same, only without the coffee. After paying for the breakfast, they bought provisions for their trip. Darby rented a carriage and they tied their saddle horses to the back of it before leaving town.

"How far is it to Denver?" Darby asked.

"About a hundred miles," Bert said with a yawn as he

curled up in his seat, laid his head on Jake's haunches and went to sleep.

"Great," Darby said, trying to get their carriage horse moving off in the right direction.

He drove through Cheyenne quickly, deciding that the best thing to do was to give the carriage horse its head as long as it kept traveling south. They passed around the giant Union Pacific trainyards that set Cheyenne apart from so many other rail towns. It was easy to find the road leading down to Denver; it was nothing more than a set of well-worn ruts marked by the litter of empty bottles, cans and occasional broken-down wagons. But less than a hundred yards off in either direction, the prairie was grassy and rolling, the day blustery and invigorating. Darby smoked cigars and watched antelope graze on the hillsides next to thousands of longhorn cattle. He supposed that, not so many years before, these same hills had been home for millions of buffalo.

Here and there Darby noticed their ancient wallows—deep, hollowed-out depressions in the earth. He could also see their bones lying bleached in the sun. With just a little stretch of his imagination he could visualize the wild, free Indians on their painted ponies, chasing after the buffalo, spearing and shooting them with arrows, glorying in the chase and the hunt that would provide food, shelter and prosperity for their tribes as it had for untold generations.

Now, all that was vanishing. The transcontinental railroad had brought progress but it also spelled the doom of the buffalo herds and the nomadic existence of the fierce Plains Indians. The Texas longhorns and the cowboys now were poised to command these millions of square miles of rolling grassland. More men and cattle were arriving every year. The word in Texas was that there was rich, free cattle country to be settled in the north, especially in Wyoming and Montana. Farmers and their families also were trying to carve a living out of this countryside. Here and there he could see a sod house and a few acres of corn, wheat or barley; but mostly this was ideal cattle country.

Change was coming fast to the Northern Plains. Darby could not help but feel a twinge of regret whenever he saw a few reservation or town Indians. Even their great leaders, such as Sitting Bull and Crazy Horse, while still practicing the old way of life, must have tasted bitterness in the knowledge that theirs was the last free generation. And in spite of their tribal customs and ceremonies, nothing could change the fact that, like the buffalo, they were a doomed people.

By the end of this first full day of travel, Bert had finished off the whiskey and was in a surly mood.

"If we don't get something to drink soon," he threatened, "I'm going to climb on my horse with Jake and ride on back to Whiskey Creek!"

"Try it," Darby warned, "and it will be the last thing you ever do."

"Oh yeah? Well, Jake will have something to say about that!"

Darby had been cultivating the dog's friendship all day and now he petted the animal and it wagged its tail and licked his hand. "I don't think so."

"Goddamn traitor!" Bert hissed.

They rode along in silence for almost an hour before Bert said, "What if the orphanage done went out of business? That wouldn't be my fault."

"I'll worry about that if and when I have to."

On the second day, they met construction crews for the newly formed Denver Pacific Railroad that was laying track up to Cheyenne. After that they ate their meals with the construction workers, paying one dollar a meal, until they arrived in Denver where they checked into the two-story brick Fairmont Hotel.

"All right," Darby said, closing the door to their hotel room after they'd smuggled Jake up the fire escape, "tell me the name of the orphanage."

"Not before you pay me half. Two hundred fifty big ones, Mr. Buckingham."

Darby shook his head. "I just don't trust you enough to do that. So, why don't we have a meal and a good night's sleep, then go track down this orphanage the first thing tomorrow morning."

"Sounds reasonable." Bert nodded his head. "Couple of steaks and a bottle of whiskey, some . . ."

"No more whiskey. A couple of beers, but that's all. And if Jake is going to stay inside with us, you're going to take him for a walk tonight before we go to bed and *no more pickled eggs!*"

"You're a hard man," Bert complained.

Darby didn't deny the fact and he didn't mind one little bit that Bert hardly spoke to him the rest of the day and evening.

That night, Darby awoke to hear Jake's tail thumping on the floor. He opened his eyes to see Bert rummaging through his coat pockets. Darby snapped into wakefulness and said, "If you don't go back to bed this instant, I'm going to put you to sleep for a long, long time."

Bert was not a man who appreciated the subtleties but he did understand the threat and he jumped back into bed. Minutes later, the old man was snoring but Darby was wide awake. He still had no idea whether or not Bert was leading him down a blind alley, although he'd know before the morning was over.

Darby could not go back to sleep and so, at dawn, he rolled groggily out of bed and got dressed. There was a small writing table next to the window overlooking Larimer Street and he found some paper and pencil. Darby began to write, something that he had not done much lately. Writing had always been therapeutic to him and now, as the words flowed, he felt his spirits lift.

I do not know what I will do if I don't find Dolly's children here. This old man with whom I am traveling would say anything for a bottle of whiskey and yet . . . despite all outward appearances and his gluttonous behavior . . . I believe that he still possesses a shred of honor and decency. Why? Because, as strange as this sounds, he loves his flatulant old dog. I think as long as a man can love something, there must be some good in his heart.

There is another reason why I believe Bert is to be trusted and that is because he hates Jim Talbot and would do anything within his power to damage the man. I believe that Talbot does not want his children to know of their parentage. After all, they were very young when they were sent away. I am sure that the orphanage was instructed that they should never know their true parents. By this cruel method, Jim and Tracy would never be in a position to claim an inheritance. And while I admit that this is all my own personal theory without benefit of fact, it makes sense and accounts for the mystery surrounding their disappearance. It seems to me that there can be no other explanation for their being sent away while they were still infants.

This being the case, I can only surmise that Jim Talbot is a heartless and bitter man. What other kind could impose such a callous fate on his own flesh and blood? If I am proven wrong, so much the better. If these children have been well provided for all these years, then I will think more kindly of Jim Talbot. However, I seriously doubt that this is the case and now I anxiously await the moment that will either vindicate my theory or prove it false.

Darby finished writing, then gazed down on Larimer Street and saw that there was already plenty of wagon traffic. The rising sun was burnishing the Rocky Mountains and the day promised to be a beautiful one if everything worked out and Dolly's children were found.

THIRTEEN

BERT HAD NOT APPRECIATED being roused out of bed shortly after daybreak, but Darby did not care. He got the old man moving, and by nine o'clock they'd had a large breakfast and enough coffee to rouse the dead.

"All right," Darby said, "where is it?"

"Hell if I know," Bert said. "All I know is that it was called the Mountain Home Orphanage."

"Good enough," Darby said, heading for the editorial offices of the Rocky Mountain News and dragging the old man along in his wake.

They pushed inside and Darby strode up to a clerk. "Is Mr. Thornton still the managing editor?"

"Why . . . why, yes. Aren't you Mr. Darby Buckingham—the famed Derby Man?"

Darby removed his derby. "I am," he said, pleased that the clerk recognized him and trying to ignore the excitement his arrival already was generating in the newspaper office.

"What a pleasure to meet you, sir! I read every one of your books."

"I'm delighted to hear that," Darby said, cheeks coloring a little, "but I am on a mission of some urgency."

"Of course. Come right this way."

Bert snickered something uncomplimentary under his bad breath but Darby ignored him. A few minutes later they were being received by William F. Thornton, one of the finest newspapermen in the West and a man whom Darby had met on several pleasant occasions during his travels through this part of the country.

"What a genuine delight to see you!" Thornton exclaimed, coming around his desk and pumping Darby's hand. "Bring any more novels?"

"I'm afraid not. Next one—*Two Fists, Two Bullets*—is coming out in about a month."

"We'll give it our usual excellent review, you can be sure."

Darby turned to Bert. "Mr. Thornton, this is Bert . . ."

"Just plain old Bert," the ex-broncbuster said, ignoring the editor's proffered hand. "And all this sugary talk is givin' me indigestion. You got anything to drink in that desk?"

"Why . . ." Thornton looked at Darby for help.

"Never mind him and his bad manners," Darby said. "We have come all the way from Whiskey Creek."

"Where?"

"It's a little nothing town on the Union Pacific line, right up in the Laramie Mountains."

"Nothing town!" Bert snorted defensively. "What do you mean by that!"

Darby clamped a hand down on Bert's shoulder and drove him into a chair. He returned his attention to the editor. "I need to find the Mountain Home Orphanage."

"The what?"

"The Mountain Home Orphanage. It was in operation, oh, seventeen or eighteen years ago."

"This town isn't much older than that." The editor scowled. "I'm afraid that there is no such establishment in Denver. If there were, I'd know about it."

Darby's heart sank. He twisted around and glared down at Bert. "Are you certain?" he asked him.

"Sure! They musta went out of business."

Darby could not be certain whether the man was lying or

not, a fact that kept him from dismantling Bert, limb by arthritic limb.

"Perhaps," Thornton said, "we could do a little research and find some reference to it. Also, there are several orphanages in Denver and it is possible that one of them used to be called the Mountain Home Orphanage."

"All right," Darby said, trying to hide his deep disappointment, "let's do the research and see what turns up."

Mr. Thornton stepped to the door of his fine office. "Mr. Ganzel! Would you come here, please?"

A rotund, rosy-cheeked young man with thin whitish-blonde hair detached himself from his office chair, quickly stuffed a pastry into his desk drawer and gulped madly before hurrying over to his editor.

"Yes, Mr. Thornton?"

"Mr. Ganzel, this is Mr. Buckingham, who I'm sure you recognize as America's most famous dime novelist, and Mr. . . . Mr. Bert. I want you to do a little research for them this morning."

"But what about that piece that . . ."

"Give it to Mr. Smith. How difficult can it be to write an article on the joys of quilting with strips of dyed gunnysack?"

Ganzel winked and rolled his eyes. "Actually, I think Richard is vastly better qualified to do the piece anyway," he confided.

"Fine, fine," Thornton said, his cheeks flushing with embarrassment. "Now, if you will listen carefully to Mr. Buckingham."

"Ahhh," Darby said, "if you don't mind, I'd like to assist the young man."

"But really," Thornton protested, "I'm sure that you can find more enjoyable tasks than poring through musty old copies of this newspaper, hoping for some reference to that orphanage."

"I'd prefer to help," Darby said. "Honest."

"Very well. And you, Mr. . . . Bert?"

"I'd like to go get drunk. You got a little spare pocket change?"

"That's enough!" Darby snapped. Turning to the shocked editor, he said, "Never mind this man. He's a little out of sorts, but finding the orphanage is every bit as important to him as it is to me. Isn't that right, Bert?"

Bert muttered something under his breath and Darby added, "And I'm sure Bert would enjoy assisting Mr. Ganzel and myself in this research."

"Hell, I can't even read!"

"Oh." Darby frowned. "Then you can come and keep us company."

Mr. Ganzel led them into a back room where they found stacks and stacks of yellowing newspapers. The young man said, "I'm afraid that there is little order and our oldest copies are on the bottoms of all the stacks."

"Naturally," Darby said, removing his coat and loosening his collar. "Mr. Ganzel, Bert, let's get down to business."

It took a full hour even to reach the bottom of the rear stacks and then another tedious four hours of scanning them to find their first clue.

"Look," Darby cried, holding up the paper, "an advertisement for the Mountain Home Orphanage!"

Even young Mr. Ganzel, who had not been told why the reference was so important, got excited. "It gives an address at 117 Lawrence Street."

"Where in blazes is that?"

"We can be there in ten minutes," Ganzel promised, "but it's not likely you'll find an orphanage anymore. That's a pretty rundown area now, with the usual unsavory establishments that cater to the beast in man."

"Let's go, anyway," Darby said.

"What about my money!" Bert demanded. "I told you the truth. It's not my fault if the damned place went out of business."

"Later," Darby said. He rushed out of the newspaper

office and down the street with Ganzel, followed closely by Bert. True to Ganzel's word, in less than ten minutes they were standing, out of breath, in front of a towering old Victorian mansion.

Darby started up the steps but Ganzel grabbed his arm. "I don't think you want to go in there."

"Why not?"

"Look." Ganzel pointed up to a window where a scantily clad young woman was motioning at them to come inside. "I think this is a house of ill repute, sir. In fact, I know it is."

"Oh." Darby frowned and bit his lower lip. "Well, all I'm buying is information. Come along, Mr. Ganzel!"

They went right up to the door and knocked loudly.

"Come on in, boys!" a woman purred, opening the door.

Darby removed his derby and the three men entered a room where three painted ladies were sitting at a very ornate bar. Their bosoms were jutting out of their low-cut dresses and their expressions looked jaded; their smiles were mechanical, their faces as pale and cold as candle wax.

"Say, big boys," the madam said, slipping out of the shadows and taking their arms. She was a very large, fleshy woman and her makeup was as thick as dried mud, cracking at the very wrinkle lines she sought to hide. "I'll just bet you men are looking for some real action."

Darby pulled his arm away. "Madam," he said, "I understand that this was once an orphanage."

"A what?"

"The Mountain Home Orphanage, to be precise."

"You want children?"

"Two, in particular, though they would be almost grown by now. It's important that I track them down."

"I can't help you that way," the woman said. "But . . ."

"How long have you been here?" Darby interrupted.

"Five years working for someone else, three years ownin'

the place." The woman's voice lost its welcome. "Why are you asking so many damned questions, big boy?"

Darby knew that he wasn't going to find out anything from this woman. "Never mind," he said, heading for the door. "Excuse us for the bother."

"Well, you don't have to rush off," the woman called. "Have a drink. Have some fun. What's the matter with you, anyway?"

Darby didn't bother to answer. He hurried back out into the street, feeling totally dejected. The others followed. "Another blind alley," Darby said to them, unable to hide his acute disappointment.

"Why don't you go talk to the other orphanages?" Ganzel suggested. "Wouldn't hurt, would it?"

"No," Darby said grudgingly, "but it probably won't help, either."

However, an hour later, Darby heard Mr. Phillip Andrews, director of the Denver Christian Orphanage, say, "Yes, the previous owner of this institution did take over the Mountain Home Orphanage and assume responsibility for all of its charges."

"Did he take custody of a brother and a sister named Jim and Tracy?"

"What were their last names?"

"Talbot."

"I'm afraid that does not ring a bell with me," the director said with a shrug of his thin shoulders.

"They might have been given different last names," Darby said. "They were brought down by . . . who did bring them down, Bert?"

Bert held out his hand for money and his jaw was set with such determination that Darby realized he must either strangle the man or pay him.

"Very well," the Derby Man said, reaching for his wallet and counting out $250 to Bert. "But if you have nothing of value to say, then you won't keep the money long enough to spend it."

Bert slipped the money into his back pocket. "Mr. Andrews, those two kids were brought to the Mountain Home Orphanage by a couple named Horton. Mr. William and Mrs. Caroline Horton."

"Hmmm. I do have possession of all the adoption records dating back to the founding of the Mountain Home Orphanage. I suppose I could go back one of these days and check."

Darby wasn't about to wait. "Mr. Andrews," he said, peeling off a hundred dollars for the director, "I'd appreciate it if you checked right now."

"My, my!" Andrews exclaimed as he plucked the cash from Darby's hand. "You really *are* eager to locate those children!"

"I sure am."

The next ten minutes, while Andrews hunted for the file, were a lifetime to Darby. "Yes, here it is! James and Tracy Horton. They were twins. There is also a scribbled note on their file card that says that Mrs. Horton was mentally unstable and that her husband was unable to care for the children because of his wife's mental condition."

"Where are they now?"

"The boy was adopted when he was ten by . . . oh, no!"

Darby's heart sank. "What's wrong this time?"

"The man who adopted Jim Horton was named John Deets."

"So?"

"So, John Deets became a famous Colorado outlaw," Andrews explained. "He and his gang were caught while trying to rob the local bank. Those that did not die in the shootout were hanged."

Darby groaned. "Is there any record of one of the gang being named Jim Horton?"

"I couldn't say for sure. You'd have to check with the sheriff—or the mortician."

Bert frowned. "This might be the end of the trail for Dolly's son."

"I know," Darby said. "He'd be old enough to join and ride with an outlaw gang. If he's one of those that died or were hanged, it's going to be devastating for Miss Beavers."

"Who is Miss Beavers?" the director asked.

"Their real mother." Darby pushed himself back up in his chair. "What about the girl?"

"Hmmm," Andrews mused, studying the file. "It seems that she was not adopted until about seven years ago by a couple up in Central City."

"And their names?"

The director's eyes skimmed over several pages of the file. "Well, this is also quite remarkable! The girl was readopted by the Hortons."

Darby didn't understand the significance of this but decided to ponder it later. "Is there anything else in that file that might help me locate Tracy?"

"No. And frankly, it would be unethical of me to tell you anything more. There is a trust of confidentiality in this business which I've already come very near to violating. But, since you have been so generous, I bent the rules."

Darby came to his feet. "If the Hortons are still in Central City, I'll find them and the girl. But first, I had better do some investigating about the boy."

"Yes. I hope that he was not a member of the Deets outlaw gang, Mr. Buckingham. It's a tragedy that such people were allowed to adopt the child. But then, we can't always screen out the bad ones. And there is no shortage of children needing to be adopted. This is such a violent country that parents are often snuffed out during their prime, leaving children without relatives to care for them."

"I understand. If young James is dead, nothing can be done about it," Darby said, picking up his derby and taking his leave.

Bert came hustling along behind. "I told you I was on the level."

"Yes, and you've been paid handsomely for your information."

"Only half."

"If I find them, you'll receive the balance," Darby promised, "even if young James is to be found in a grave."

Satisfied, Bert said no more as the two of them walked to the sheriff's office. Inside, Darby quickly explained his mission. "I just need to know if the young man was a member of the Deets gang or not."

"If he was, he escaped," the sheriff said. "There were no dead boys after the gunsmoke cleared and the pair we caught and hanged were half-breeds."

Darby felt a mixture of relief and disappointment, and he knew that he was now back at the beginning with no leads to follow.

"Thank you," he said, "and by the way, have you ever heard of a family named the Hortons living in Central City?"

"Nope. They might have moved on to another strike. You see, in the early sixties, Central City rivaled Denver Town and had a population of over ten thousand. I know, because that's where I got my start as a lawman. But when the gold petered out, population dwindled and I got laid off. I was real lucky to get on here and I worked my way into bein' the town sheriff."

"Well, congratulations," Darby said.

"Yes sir, Mr. Derby Man," the sheriff told him, "it's just like that old sayin'."

"What saying?"

"That the cream always rises."

Darby nodded and shook the man's hand. As he left he felt quite pessimistic about his chances of finding Tracy if Central City was in such rapid decline.

"That sheriff was a real blowhard, wasn't he?" Bert grumped as he hurried along beside the Derby Man. "He sure liked to gong his own bell."

"Let's get our horses and ride on up to Central City. If we leave now, maybe we can be there before dark."

"Fat damn chance."

Darby set his jaw and headed for the livery. From the moment he'd awakened this day, he'd felt his emotions in turmoil, one minute up, the next down. And if he came up empty in Central City, he would be no closer to finding Dolly's children than he had been the day he bid the poor woman goodbye. That being the case, he would be praying for a telegram from Austin Applegate.

If Austin also came up empty in Reno with Whiskey Creek's former "two-dollar woman," things were going to be very bleak indeed.

FOURTEEN

WHEN AUSTIN wearily stepped down from the train in Reno, a slender man with the look of a gunfighter moved onto the passenger platform and pretended to look around, as if expecting someone. When Austin collected his bag and headed into town on foot, the man rolled a cigarette, glanced around once more and followed him.

Austin was not sure where he would start looking for Miss Puddingstone but he did have a few ideas. The first was that a respectable woman would seek a ladies' boarding house where gentlemen were allowed to visit only during certain hours and under strict supervision. At least, that was how it was done back East.

"Excuse me," he said, doffing his derby to a matronly-looking woman in her forties, "but do you know the whereabouts of the nearest ladies' boarding house?"

Her eyebrows shot up. "I certainly do not!" She raised her chin and huffed off down the street.

"Well," Austin said to himself, "I guess that I've been put in my place."

A few minutes later, however, he tried again, this time with a very pretty young lady about his own age. Sweeping his hat off with a flourish, he bowed slightly and said, "Dear lady, can you tell me where I might find the nearest boarding house for single women?"

She wore a gray dress and her hair was drawn back

rather severely in a little brown bun. "And just what are your intentions?"

"I am . . ." Austin said, "searching for a woman named Miss Dora Puddingstone, recently arrived in this fair city."

"I see. Is she . . ."

"An acquaintance," he said, "nothing more."

"Well," the girl said, "my name is Miss Walker and it just so happens I know Miss Puddingstone. She lives in our boarding house, the finest in Reno."

"May I inquire as to its location?"

"Better than that," she said, taking his arm, "you may escort me there, Mr. . . ."

"Applegate. Austin Applegate."

They chatted on the way to the boarding house, and although the girl was very helpful, Austin's mind was totally fixed on his crucial meeting with Miss Dora Puddingstone. He was vastly relieved that the former Whiskey Creek woman was still in Reno. Had she moved on, Austin had resolved to track her down even if that required his going all the way to San Francisco.

They stopped at the boarding house door. Miss Walker said, "I'm afraid that visiting hours aren't until six o'clock this evening."

"But I must see Miss Puddingstone at once."

"That's just not possible. But it's one o'clock now and . . ."

Austin didn't hear the rest because he opened the door and marched inside. The parlor was empty except for a large, matronly woman who was arranging a vase of flowers. When she saw Austin, her pleasant expression took on a decided chill.

"Sir, can't you read the sign posted on the door? You are not allowed to call until . . ."

"I know. I know. But this is something of an emergency. I must see Miss Puddingstone right now!"

"No, you must leave right now."

Miss Walker scooted around Austin and planted herself

beside the older woman. "Mrs. Bates, I told him the rule. I should never have brought such a man here," she said nervously. "But he seemed . . ."

"Never mind," Austin said with exasperation. "I'll wait outside. It is permissible for Miss Puddingstone to meet me outside, isn't it?"

"Of course. And you needn't be impertinent, young man!" Mrs. Bates snapped.

"Then tell her that Austin Applegate must talk to her right now."

The two women glared at Austin but he paid them no mind as he retreated outside. He began to pace nervously back and forth in front of the boarding house, totally oblivious of the lean gunfighter who watched from across the street.

At last Miss Puddingstone appeared, looking very angry.

"Damn you, Austin!" she hissed as she grabbed his arm and pulled him behind the screen of some shrubbery. "Now you're going to have everyone talking about me and my ungentlemanly visitor! Why couldn't you just wait until six o'clock like everyone else who calls!"

"Because," he said, "I've been riding a train for three days in anticipation of this moment. You're the only one who might be able to help us find Dolly's children. We seem to have come to a dead end."

"Let them go!" she said angrily. "What good can come of stirring up the past? Did Dolly put you up to this?"

"No! Well, they are the reason she came back."

"That's her problem now. Besides, Dolly never even knew those children."

"But she wants to know them now!"

"I don't give a damn what she wants!"

Austin curbed his anger. He forced himself to realize that it was hopeless to try to evoke sympathy in this woman for her old childhood friend. "If you won't help me for Dolly's sake," he said, "then at least do it for the children.

You must have felt something for them while they were in your care."

"Of course, I did! I thought I was going to be raising them," she said bitterly. "I cared for them deeply."

"Then help them now," Austin pleaded. "Otherwise, they'll never share in Talbot's wealth. That's the sole reason he banished them to some orphanage after you left the Rocking T. Are you going to allow that man to deny those children their rightful inheritance?"

She started to leave him but Austin grabbed her arm.

"Let go of me or I'll scream!"

"Listen, please. Jim Talbot cheated you for years. He promised that someday he'd marry you and give you the Talbot name."

"Damn the Talbot name!"

"Then how about its wealth and power? The man cheated you and then drove you away, just as he drove Dolly away. Are you willing to see him do the same to his own flesh and blood? Somewhere there are two children who were sent off to a wretched orphanage, never knowing who their parents were or from whence they came. That just isn't right! It isn't any more fair than what the man did to you and to Dolly." Austin released the woman's arm. "If you don't help, Jim Talbot will have beaten every last one of you! Is that how you want it to end?"

The woman shook her head and slumped against the building as the anger suddenly drained away. "I just want to put it all behind me," she whispered. "I just want to forget the whole nightmare. My sordid past. Everything. I've already attracted a good, honest man."

"I couldn't be happier," Austin said, meaning it, "but I helped you become Miss Puddingstone. I gave you a chance to start fresh. Now you must help me give those children a chance."

Tears sprang to her eyes. She sniffled and took his arm. "Walk a little with me," she said, leading Austin off the porch and out into a rose garden where they could be seen but not heard.

She motioned for him to sit on a small marble bench in the garden. She breathed deeply of the fragrance of the flowers and that seemed to revive her spirit. "I can't tell you how happy I am now," she said. "I feel like I've come alive for the first time since I was a girl. I feel good inside, Austin."

"You look wonderful."

Her eyes brimmed and she studied the roses. "Austin, you should see the way that Mr. Ross looks at me! He's in love. *He* doesn't quite know it yet, but I do. And he'll ask me to marry him within the month."

Austin nodded. This was not the desperate, haunted woman he remembered from Whiskey Creek.

"Austin," she was saying, "please don't misunderstand me, but I don't ever want to see you again. I owe you so much but you are part of my past that I just want to forget. If I tell you what I know, will you promise never to come back to visit me again?"

"I do."

"Or tell anyone my new name or identity?"

"I swear silence until death."

She took a deep breath and sat down at his side. "All right, then. I know but little. The last I heard, Tracy was growing up in Central City, Colorado."

"And her twin brother?"

"I'm afraid that he will come to a bad end. He was adopted by an outlaw and might have taken the outlaw trail."

"Where can I find him?"

"I heard that he was living in the Colorado Rockies someplace north of Central City."

Austin shook his head. "That's not going to help me much."

"He was working for a packer handling mules and pack-strings that supplied the mining camps. I heard he was in love with the man's daughter, a half-breed girl whose mother was a full-blooded Ute."

"That's all? No last name or anything?" Austin could not hide his disappointment. He had expected much, much more.

Dora Puddingstone thought hard for a moment. "I'm sorry. But from what I've told you, it shouldn't be that hard to find the man and his family, should it?"

"I suppose not," Austin said, trying to hide his disappointment, "although a young man changes sweethearts about as fast as he changes his shirt."

"That might be true, but I heard that young Jim was crazy for this girl. I have a feeling that, if he didn't marry her, he would always be in love with her, for she was his first real love. Men never forget their first loves, Mr. Applegate. Take it from me, a woman who would know."

"Thank you," Austin said. "And I wish you a long and happy life as Mrs. Ross."

"I have a chance," she told him, "and since it was you that gave it to me, I am giving one in return."

Austin nodded and hurried away. The gunfighter watched him and stayed until Dora Puddingstone went into the boarding house. He came up to the porch, started to go inside and then saw the posted rules. He turned and followed Austin, determined to keep his quarry in sight.

Austin checked into the Riverfront Hotel and was instantly greeted as a celebrity because of his association with the Derby Man. Austin was sure that they were all wild to ask him about Darby's search to find Dolly, but he felt that this information was privileged and so he said nothing.

After a hot bath, a shave and a change of clothes, Austin went out and had an excellent trout dinner. By the time he started back to the hotel, his mind still swirling with the information he'd obtained from Miss Puddingstone, the evening was growing late. He paused on the bridge overlooking the Truckee and gazed down at the water. The lights from the city reflected off the flowing water and the effect charmed him.

"Don't make a sound or a false move," a voice said behind him.

Austin started to turn but froze when he felt a gun barrel jammed into his ribs.

"Who are you?"

"None of your business. Start walking."

"Where are we going?"

"Under the bridge," the man said. "We're going to have a little talk."

Austin shivered. He had a premonition that if they went under the bridge he would never emerge from there alive. And yet, to refuse to go would mean a quick bullet.

"Walk!" the man hissed.

Austin turned and started to walk very slowly. He wished he could see the gunman's face. His voice sounded quite young. They crossed the bridge; there was a steep, thirty-foot incline leading down to the water. It seemed his only hope of escape.

"Who are you?" he asked, taking a tentative step down the trail. "If you just want money, then . . ."

"Shut up!"

Austin took a deep breath and another step. He pretended that his feet slipped out from under him and he fell heavily. The man with the gun cursed and grabbed his arm to haul him back to his feet. That was exactly the break Austin needed. He grabbed the arm and yanked with all of his might. A tremendous explosion sounded beside his ear, and for one blinding instant Austin was sure that his brains had been blown apart.

The man was falling past him, firing in every direction as he dragged Austin tumbling down the incline to crash into the freezing Truckee River. The water was so cold it almost stopped Austin's racing heart. The coldness grabbed his throat and squeezed the breath right out of him just before he slipped under the surface of the black, roiling water. He struck the bottom of the river and the powerful current spun him completely around. Churning wildly, Austin broke the surface, saw nothing but darkness and shouted, "Help!"

His cry brought another explosion and he realized the gunman was only a few feet away and they were being swept under the Virginia Street Bridge. Austin ducked under the water, held his breath and let the current rush him along. When he surfaced again, his assailant was thrashing toward him with the gun.

Austin was a good swimmer but he knew flight was not the answer. He recognized the gunman's face as a fellow train passenger from Whiskey Creek. Before, the man had looked quite unassuming and harmless. Now his expression was crazed. Self-preservation made Austin double up his fists and lash out with all his strength.

The man hit him back but Austin was already numb from the cold. They locked and twisted back under the dark water. Beating at each other's faces, they spiraled into the coldest, darkest pockets of the frigid river.

Lungs threatening to explode, they broke apart and clawed back to the surface. They were fully dressed and the water seemed to grab their legs and pull them down. Austin, with his breath whooshing in and out of his mouth and his strength ebbing away, remembered Darby's advice and drove his fist toward his opponent's exposed throat. The man grabbed his neck and began to choke. Austin fumbled for his derringer but his opponent's head sank from sight.

It did not appear again.

FIFTEEN

CENTRAL CITY, Colorado, was a hard thirty-mile climb into the towering Rockies west of Denver. Old Hallelujah wasn't fit for the high altitude and kept stopping every few hundred yards for a long breather.

"At this rate," Darby complained, "we'll be lucky to reach Central City by tomorrow night!"

"You got plenty of money," Bert said, adjusting Jake to a more comfortable position on the saddle. "Get rid of that damned plug and buy a young, strong horse like this buckskin."

Darby knew that he ought to take Bert's advice. Hallelujah just wasn't up to a long mountain climb but Darby had grown comfortable with the beast and felt a shred of loyalty.

That night, when they stopped at a small hostelry and Darby was just about to enjoy a platter piled high with steak and mashed potatoes awash in gravy, Bert appeared with a horse trader.

"Darby, this here is Slade. He buys and sells horses. I thought you might want to do some horse trading."

"Well, I don't," Darby said, tired and hungry from his travels.

"Now see here, Buckingham. You're a dude so you don't understand that a big man like you needs a draft-type horse. I've exactly that kind of animal," the rough-looking horse trader said, "and I'm ready to deal."

"I'll just bet you are. But I'll keep Hallelujah. It's only ten or twelve more miles up to Central City and our return journey will be downhill."

Slade wasn't listening. "You see, Buckingham, a horse that is not used to high country can develop heart problems. Now, you don't want to be responsible for killing a good flatland horse, do you?"

"Of course not! Now, if you'll excuse me while I finish my dinner . . ."

"Man, you need to open your ears instead of your mouth! I'm willing to sell you a big horse in mountain condition for just fifty dollars more than that flatland crowbait you're riding." Slade banged his hand down on the table hard enough to spill Darby's beer. "Use your head!"

The Derby Man carefully wiped his lips and mustache with his napkin, then stood to confront Slade. The horse trader was taller by several inches but not as thick in the chest and shoulders.

"This discussion is closed."

The man's lower lip dropped in contempt and a curse fouled his breath. Darby's hands jumped up from his sides and he crushed Slade's ears in both fists, then jerked the horse trader's face down into the steaming mashed potatoes and gravy.

Slade roared, slapping wildly at his face and trying to clear his eyes.

Darby released the man's ears and planted his right fist in Slade's face. The man backpedaled wildly across the floor, and when he hit the opposite wall the entire room shook. Slade squatted on the carpet and feebly tried to clear his eyes of potatoes and gravy. The roomful of miners and freighters stared first at the horse trader, then at Darby.

"This here is my friend Mr. Darby Buckingham!" Bert

announced to the stunned audience. "Better known as the Derby Man!"

Darby bowed slightly. Being somewhat fastidious, he dabbed at the potatoes and gravy on his stinging knuckles, then signaled the waiter to bring a fresh platter.

"I'd like to get an early start tomorrow morning," Darby said. "I hope that you'll be in condition to come along."

Darby's meaning was very clear and Bert nodded his head. "Don't you worry," he vowed, "I'll be ready."

"Good," Darby said, tucking his napkin back into his collar and sipping his fresh glass of beer.

They topped a final divide early the next afternoon and saw the sprawling mining town of Central City. Stamping mills powered by huge steam engines pounded rock into powder and shook the valley. Smoke floated a dirty haze over the settlement, and the landscape, as far as Darby could see, was littered with mine tailings.

Central City was actually quite impressive from a distance. There were dozens of big brick buildings and a main street that was a good quarter of a mile long. And despite what the sheriff had told them, the streets were clotted with the wagons of commerce.

"Quite a place," Darby remarked as they started down into the smokey mountain metropolis.

"I hope Tracy is there so I can get paid," Bert said. "Be nice to start off for Mexico before the snows begin to fall in this high country."

Darby gave no sign that he was listening. All of his concentration was focused on the city below, which he guessed still had a population of at least seven or eight thousand. Over and over, he kept asking himself if Tracy was still here. Darby realized he didn't even know what the girl looked like, although he had a hunch she would bear more than a passing resemblance to her beautiful mother.

And what if she were married? Perhaps even had children? This was a serious possibility that he had not considered, he now realized. And, God forbid, what if she had become a lady of the night? What would he say or do? How could he possibly tell Dolly? The Derby Man was reminded again of Bert's comment that finding these two "orphans" might cause more sorrow than joy.

So it was that Darby's expectancy was tempered with more than a little apprehension as they rode into Central City. He reined Hallelujah in before the sheriff's office and stiffly dismounted.

"You coming in with me?" he asked Bert.

"I'll wait. If she's here we'll be ridin' someplace, and if she ain't we'll also be ridin' someplace. I'm getting too old to be liftin' Jake on and off this tall buckskin."

Darby tied up his horse and went inside. The sheriff was gone but there was a smiling deputy. After Darby introduced himself, he came right to the point. "Do you know a young woman named Tracy Horton?"

"Of course. Everyone knows her. Miss Tracy is a celebrity here."

"A celebrity?"

"She's easily the most popular dance-hall girl in Central City. Works at the Ace High Saloon just a block up the street. Can't miss it."

"She's a dance-hall girl?"

"Yep. Dances on the bar and on the stage. Sings a little, but not too good. Truth is, nobody cares 'cause she's so pretty. Why you lookin' for Miss Horton?"

"It's a long story," Darby said, turning to leave before the man could ask him any more questions. He hurried outside, and since it was only a block to the Ace High, Darby untied Hallelujah and began to lead the horse down the street, ignoring Bert's look of disgust.

"You want to come in and meet her?" Darby asked.

"Why not?"

Bert dismounted and helped Jake down. The dog wagged its tail and seemed to know that they were going inside a saloon. It licked its chops, probably thinking of pickled eggs.

"Seems to me," Bert said, "it's time I was fully paid."

"I'll pay you tomorrow."

"Why wait?"

"Why not?" Darby asked in return. "You've got two hundred and fifty dollars of my money in your pocket. If it's drinking and gambling you crave, that ought to be enough for tonight."

"More'n enough. But like I said, I got a strong itch to get on down to Old Mexico."

"It'll hold," Darby said. "Let's see if Tracy is inside."

The moment he stepped into the Ace High, Darby knew he was looking at Tracy. She was leaning against a piano and singing a popular miners' ballad called "The Girl with the Gold Nugget Heart."

Darby had heard the song before and thought it maudlin to the extreme but he scarcely paid any attention to the lyrics as he studied Tracy. Not only did she have Dolly's heart-shaped face, voluptuous figure and golden locks, but she had the same lousy singing voice that broke on the high notes and quivered like a defective bowstring on the low ones.

"Why, girl," Bert exclaimed, walking right up to Tracy and squinting like a rodent, "you are the spittin' image of your mama!"

Tracy forgot the lyrics. The piano player kept pounding his keys and a few of the customers who had been listening complained, but otherwise, no one seemed to notice.

"Mister, who are you?" Tracy asked when she had regained her composure.

"Miss Horton," Darby said, removing his derby. "Allow me to introduce myself. My name is Darby Buckingham and this is my friend Bert."

Tracy wasn't a bit impressed. "Can't either you or this blind old gopher see that I was right in the middle of a song?"

"Sincere apologies," Darby said, "but you must understand that we have come searching for you all the way from Whiskey Creek, Wyoming."

"Why?"

"Could we have a few minutes of your time so that we could talk in private?"

The girl sized him up with suspicion in her deep blue eyes. "Why?"

Darby decided to be very direct. "I am aware that you were raised in a Denver orphanage. I'm a friend of your real mother."

Tracy's face drained of color and she stared. "Who are *you?* My real father?"

"No. As I said, I am a friend of your mother."

"I don't believe a word of this!"

"Perhaps I can change your mind," Darby said, reaching into his pocket and removing his monogrammed leather wallet. He handed Bert $250 to signal that their agreement was concluded; then he located a daguerreotype of Dolly Beavers and silently offered it to the girl.

Tracy's breath caught in her throat as she stared at the picture, nearly a mirror image of herself.

"Your mother's maiden name is Dolly Beavers," Darby said, taking the girl's arm and leading her away from the noisy piano and out through the front door. The bartender called something to Tracy but she was too stunned to hear or acknowledge the man, and Darby led her down the boardwalk until they were standing alone at the edge of town.

"Miss Horton," Darby said, "I know this must come as a terrible shock."

"Why did she . . . she leave me?" Tracy whispered.

"It's a long story and rather a sad one. Believe me, until a very short time ago I knew as little of this as yourself. You see, I am your mother's fiancé."

Tracy's pretty mouth crimped and her voice trembled. "My mother is dead. At least, to me she is."

Darby led the girl over to a hitched but empty wagon. He picked her up as easily as if she were a doll, then he set her down on the wagonbed. "Dear girl, perhaps I should begin at the beginning, many years ago."

"I'm not sure that I want to know about her," Tracy whispered. "I always believed that my mother had taken ill and *had* to give me away. That's what the Hortons said before they died last winter of the fever. Mr. Buckingham, are you trying to say my mother didn't want me?"

Darby removed his derby. He mopped his brow and drew a Cuban from his coat pocket. "Your mother," he began, "has longed for you every day of your life. She has wanted to hold and love you always, but your father made that impossible."

Tracy had been staring at the mountains but now her head twisted around sharply. "How could that be!"

Darby lit his cigar. "What I have to tell you is not easy. And when I'm finished, if you never want to see your mother again, then I'm sure that she will understand and respect those wishes. But first, you need to listen."

The girl nodded. She seemed to be in shock, which was not surprising to Darby, who could not imagine what his own emotions would be under the same circumstances.

Darby told the story as best he understood it. He told Tracy how Dolly had been young and vulnerable, how her father had been ambushed by the Talbots and how Dolly had fled the Rocking T Ranch. He told her also how, years later, she had risked everything in the vain hope that she might learn the whereabouts of her daughter and son.

"I have a brother!"

"A twin brother," Darby said. "I don't know where he is to be found. Unfortunately, Tracy, your brother was raised by an outlaw and might have chosen an outlaw's life."

"This is like a dream," she whispered. "After all these years, it's like I'm waking up from a dream. The Hortons always told me that my real father was rich, a big rancher who lived in Wyoming, and that someday they'd help me inherit a huge ranch."

This admission told Darby what he had already guessed about the Hortons. "No doubt they always coveted possession of the Rocking T Ranch."

"I suppose. But until now I never believed their story. I remember asking them exactly who my father and mother were, but they would never really tell. Finally, I decided that it was all just talk. They talked about it right up to the day they died."

"It wasn't just talk," Darby said. "Your father *is* a rich and powerful Wyoming rancher. He is also a very heartless man who, for some vindictive reason, refuses to acknowledge that he has children."

"I would never want to see him if he didn't want to see me."

"Understandable. But your mother has missed you desperately all these years. Will you come and meet her?"

"Where?"

"In Whiskey Creek."

"But what could we possibly say to each other after all these years? We're strangers."

"That would quickly change. Your mother is a wonderful, loving woman. I think you would be very glad to meet her."

Tracy slipped off the wagonbed. "I don't know," she said with a shake of her head. "I need to think about it."

"Of course you do," Darby said, "I will stay here for however long you need to decide."

That evening in the Ace High Saloon, Tracy sang, danced and laughed as if she hadn't a care in this world. Darby could not help but watch with a great sense of something akin to paternal pride. After all, if he had met Dolly twenty years earlier, this girl might have been their child. He wished Dolly could have been here to share his pride, and he recalled that, when he'd first met Dolly, she had been an entertainer in her own hotel and saloon in Running Springs, Wyoming. Darby had a very strong hunch that the two women would have a great deal in common. To him, they seemed more like sisters than mother and daughter.

Early the next morning, Darby met Bert at the livery to get their horses and to buy another for the girl. The liveryman wasn't up and about yet and so they waited out behind the barn, sizing up the available horses.

"Don't you think you ought to wait and see if she's going to come before you buy her a horse?" Bert asked.

"She'll come," Darby said confidently. "If she's anything at all like her mother, she couldn't do otherwise. Curiosity would eat her alive."

"It'd sort of eat me, too."

"What does that mean?"

"Means that I've been doing a little thinking. I reckon you're going to need my help in Whiskey Creek."

"But what about Old Mexico?"

Bert reached down to scratch Jake behind the ears. "I just figure Mexico can wait. This whole business is getting pretty interesting. I'd always wonder how it all worked out if I was to ride south just now."

"It's going to work out fine," Darby said with more confidence than he really felt. "Assuming we can get an early start, we'll reach Denver before nightfall. Tomorrow morning I'm going to stop at the telegraph office and find out if Austin Applegate has sent us any information on Tracy's missing brother."

"And if he hasn't?"

"Then we'll ride north to Cheyenne and then on to Whiskey Creek," Darby said. "The main thing right now is to get Tracy and her mother back together again."

"I got a strong hunch that Jim Talbot isn't going to be too damn happy about that."

"Tough," Darby snapped. "The way I see it . . ."

The ominous click of a gun's hammer being drawn back caused Darby's words to trail off into silence.

"Freeze!" a voice behind them commanded.

Darby froze. He felt his heart begin to pound. "What is this, a holdup?"

"Sure," the voice said. "As long as I'm going to shoot you, might as well take your money."

"Why?" Darby asked, wishing he could at least see the gunman.

"Why? Well, let's just say that you've been nosin' into business that is none of your concern and now you're about to get your snout chopped off."

"He's one of Talbot's men," Bert said. "This ain't no holdup."

"Shut up, Bert! You've been warned for years about your big mouth. An old man like you should have learned better after having worked so many years for the Rocking T."

Darby heard the low rumble in Jake's throat but so did the gunman.

"Tell that dog of yours to settle down, Bert!"

"Git him!"

Darby's hand was already slipping inside his coat for his derringer and when Jake attacked, Darby yanked the gun out, dove to the ground and rolled as bullets split the chill morning silence. Darby saw Jake with his fangs locked on the gunman's calf. The dog was bleeding but it was hanging on. Bert was down and the gunman was trying to take aim but the dog was giving him fits. Darby stopped rolling and fired. He missed, swore, fired a second time and the gunman crashed over backward with the dog still worrying his torn leg.

"Bert!"

Darby rushed to the old man's side. He was relieved to see that Bert was still alive, though he'd taken a slug in the shoulder. Picking the man up, Darby began to run back up the street, yelling for a doctor.

Within ten minutes, Bert was on a table and a competent-looking doctor about Darby's age was preparing to extract the bullet.

"His health isn't that good," Darby warned.

"I can see that."

"Do you think he'll live?"

The doctor thumbed back the ex-broncbuster's eyelids. "He's in shock and he's lost plenty of blood, but I think he has a good fighting chance."

Darby said a silent prayer and left the room. He hurried back to the livery where a crowd was gathered around the dead gunman. Jake was gone.

"Did anybody see a red dog with a bullet wound?" Darby asked anxiously.

"Yeah," a man called. "He's lyin' over there in that pile of straw."

Darby rushed over and found Jake but it was too late; the animal was dead.

"Blast!" Darby whispered, picking the dog up and carrying it off to be buried.

Telling Bert about his poor dog was one of the hardest things Darby had ever done. "I'm sorry."

Bert nodded and struggled to keep his composure. "He was just a barnyard dog. Nothing but a mongrel."

"He saved our lives," Darby said.

"I suspect he did," Bert said. His face was almost colorless and he was shaking for whiskey but not asking for any.

"You look in need of a drink," Darby said.

"I am but I won't take one."

Darby's eyebrows arched in surprise and Bert said, "Doc told me while he was digging that bullet out that I'd be better off to die quick of a bullet than to die of the drink."

"He said that?"

"Yep. He laid it out real plain and I could see it was up to me. I could have died if I'd a'wanted to."

"But you didn't want to."

"No," Bert said. "It struck me that I just wasn't ready yet."

"So, you're quitting the bottle?"

"I am. Otherwise, I figure Jake died for nothing."

"That's true." Darby was delighted by this change of heart. "I'm really glad that you're going to be all right."

"There might be other men come to kill us," Bert warned. "You thought of that, Mr. Derby Man?"

"I have."

"What about Miss Tracy?"

"She's coming back to Wyoming with us."

"Then I guess that I'm the one holding things up."

"We'll wait," Darby promised. "We'll head for Denver when the doctor tells us you're fit for travel and not a moment earlier."

"Thanks," Bert said. "And thanks for buryin' old Jake."

"As I said, I owe him my life."

"Yeah," Bert sighed. "I never seen man nor beast that loved pickled eggs like old Jake."

Darby had a ready rejoinder but he chose not to use it. Instead, he turned his thoughts to the dangers they might face in the days ahead—for if Talbot had sent one gunman to follow their trail, he may well have sent several others. They might be here in Central City, waiting for a second chance to use their guns, or they might be planning an ambush in Denver.

The Derby Man was worried, not so much for his own life but for Bert's and especially for Tracy's. It seemed obvious now that Talbot would stop at nothing.

SIXTEEN

"ARE THERE any telegrams waiting for Mr. Darby Buckingham?"

The Denver telegraph operator glanced up from his newspaper and stared at Darby through a set of brass bars. "Who?"

"Darby Buckingham. I'm expecting a telegram from a Mr. Austin Applegate in Reno."

The man shook his head and then went back to his newspaper, mumbling, "I don't remember one."

"Would you please look? It might have arrived a few days ago. It might also have been received by another operator. It's very important."

The man glanced up again. He was in his early forties, thin and pockmarked. "Listen, mister, I said it ain't here!"

Darby grabbed the brass bars with both hands and began to pull them apart. The bars were as thick as his middle finger. His neck sank down into his shoulders and his eyes bulged as his massive arms quivered, and then, slowly, the bars separated.

The telegraph operator's eyes bulged with disbelief and he whispered, "Oh, for . . ."

The man's oath was terminated abruptly when the Derby Man's fists bit into his shirt front. He pulled the operator over the top of his telegraph keys and table, jerking his head through the brass bars. Before the man quite knew what was happening, Darby, with a Herculean effort, squeezed the bars shut again. Caught like a rabbit in a noose, the telegraph operator screamed in panic. Darby stepped back to watch the man kick and struggle helplessly.

"When you are ready to cooperate," Darby said mildly, "I'll consider freeing you. Until then . . ."

"Please!" the man cried, shaking the bars. "Let me go!"

Darby lit a cigar. He did not take satisfaction in this pitiful and humiliating spectacle. However, there were individuals who just had to learn the hard way.

"Will you do a thorough search of your files for that telegram?"

"No, damn you!"

"In that case," Darby said, turning on his heel, "I will return later and speak to someone more reasonable."

"Wait!" the man shrilled. "Please! You can't do this to me!"

"I can and I have," Darby said, turning and surveying his handiwork.

"I . . . I'll help you! I'll apologize for my behavior. I'm sorry, Mr. Buckingham! Have mercy!"

"All right," Darby said because he had never been one to hold a grudge. He wagged his thick forefinger in the man's face. "But if you change your mind and try to fool me, you'll be very sorry."

"No! I swear I won't. If the telegram is here, I'll find it!"

"Excellent!"

Darby gripped the bars and bent his knees a little. His lips pulled back from his teeth and he puffed faster on the Cuban until he drew the bars apart once again.

The telegraph operator reeled backward, gasping as if he had been strangled instead of only snared. "Could you . . . please . . . fix them?"

"Oh, all right." Darby squeezed the bars until they were nearly straight again, all the while watching as the telegraph operator conducted a search.

"Here!" the man shouted, whipping the telegram up and waving it jubilantly. "This is it!"

Darby snapped his fingers with impatience. "Thank you very much," he said, hurrying away as his eyes scanned the message which had been sent a week earlier from Nevada: WILL BE ARRIVING IN DENVER ASAP. STOP. HAVE LEAD ON OUTLAW SON. STOP. DO NOT LEAVE TOWN. STOP.

"That's all he tells me!" Darby bellowed. "What lead?"

Darby was furious but helpless. He stomped back to their horses. "We've got no choice but to wait until Mr. Applegate arrives," he told his two companions.

"Who is he?" Tracy asked.

Darby sighed. "Austin deserves more of an explanation than I can provide at the moment. Why don't I tell you about him over dinner tonight."

That evening Darby told the young woman all about his erstwhile young protégé. When he was finished, Tracy said, "Besides being rich, and foolish enough to leave his family, is he handsome?"

"Handsome?" Darby frowned. "I suppose he would be attractive to a young woman. Of course, he's much too skinny to engender much respect on a physical level, but he is resourceful and courageous."

"I can hardly wait to meet him," Tracy said. "But, like you, I also wish that he had told us what he knows about my brother."

"Perhaps he feared that Talbot or one of his men would bribe the telegraph operators."

"My father," Tracy said, looking troubled, "sounds like an awful man."

"He's ruthless," Bert agreed. "As cold-blooded as a damned rattler."

Tracy said nothing but Darby could see that she was bothered by this description. He wished that Bert would be a little more careful in his use of words. The old cowboy was healing slowly and, so far at least, winning his struggle against alcohol, but he was about as blunt as a hammer.

They waited another week for Austin to arrive; when he did, he looked excited and very fit. "And this," Austin cried, striding across the lobby of their hotel late one afternoon, "must be your fiancée's lovely daughter! What a flower she is!"

"Oh dear," Tracy whispered to Darby, "he's going to be big trouble."

"Completely harmless," Darby assured her.

"That's what *you* think."

Darby had to wonder if she knew something that he did not. Austin was pleasant and well dressed, but he had no muscle to speak of and was not physically imposing. Even so, it was obvious that Tracy was impressed. Darby had some difficulty getting them to stop chattering niceties while he tried to pin Austin down to specifics.

"Where exactly is that brother to be found?"

Austin told him about the mule packer's half-breed daughter who lived up in the mountains. "Their ranch is supposed to be just north of Central City."

"But that's where we just came from!"

"How could I have known that?" Austin asked. "And even if I had known it, how could I have gotten that information to you?"

"Good point," Darby conceded. "So, I guess we had better return and see if we can find the young man."

"I guess so," Austin said as his eyes played with Tracy's.

"And, by the way," Darby said peevishly, "Bert and I were almost executed by one of Talbot's gunmen."

"You, too?"

"What does that mean?"

"Just that I was set upon by a gunman while crossing the Virginia Street Bridge over the Truckee. We had a very cold swim which I was lucky to survive."

"Did you recognize the gunman as being on Talbot's payroll?"

"No. And, unfortunately, the man drowned so I had no chance to pin him to the Rocking T Ranch."

"We had better be careful," Darby said to the others, "and I'll give this search no more than a couple of days. After that, I'm heading back to Whiskey Creek. Dolly is my main concern and it's time that her nightmare ended."

High in the Rocky Mountains near a log cabin and a corral full of pack mules, Jim sat next to a half-breed girl, whittling a stick. Overhead, the sky was a deep indigo with huge fluffy white clouds sailing westward like a fleet of Spanish galleons.

The girl beside him was very pretty, with large dark eyes and hair the color of mahogany wood.

"Jim," she said after a long silence, "I think that if you ride with Mace Halloran and his gang to rob that bank down in Cripple Creek, you will be killed."

He continued to whittle methodically as he turned the stick in his big callused hands. "Estella," he said in a quiet voice, "even though I never rode with the Deets Gang, everyone thinks that I did. If there isn't a reward on my head now, there will be. So, if I'm considered an outlaw, then I might as well be one."

"That's crazy thinking!" the girl protested in exasperation. "We need to go away now. That way, we could get married and start over together."

"With what?" he asked, looking up at her. "We got nothing but the clothes on our backs."

"I don't care! You're expert with horses. You could easily find work cowboying or driving a team. Or you could pack mules like you do for my father."

"I just don't know," he said, shaking his head back and forth. "It's no way for us to start out. I always said that I wouldn't ask your father for your hand unless there was something that I could offer."

"But you said so yourself—it's not safe for you in Colorado," she argued softly. "So let's just go! My father will understand."

"No," Jim said, "I don't think he will. When he returns from Cripple Creek, he'll refuse his permission."

"Then I'll marry you anyway."

"I don't want to come between you and your father. He's too good a man to cross. You're mighty important to him."

Estella touched his cheek with her fingertips. "My father has my mother. They've got each other. Just like we have each other."

Jim frowned with concentration and kept whittling until his stick was nothing but a white nubbin, which he dropped between his boots among the pile of shavings. With exaggerated care he folded his barlow knife and slipped it into his pocket.

"I just don't know," he said. "I always wanted you to have better."

"Oh, Jim," she whispered, "if you love me, don't go with those men. The same thing could happen to them as happened to John Deets and his gang."

He reached into the pockets of his patched and faded Levis. He drew out a few crumpled bills and a little change, which he counted. "Look at this, Estella," he told her with a shake of his head, "three dollars and forty-seven cents. That's all the money I have in this world."

"But there are always jobs for men good with mules or horses."

"Sure," he said, "and I could go mustanging, too. But then I'd hardly ever see you. You'd be stuck working twelve, fourteen hours a day cooking at some ranch in between doing the cleaning and laundry for the boss's wife and children. I've seen it happen again and again to the wife of a poor cowboy. Uh-uh, Estella, I ain't going to let anybody work you to death. You deserve better."

"I won't live off stolen money," she told him. "At least the other way is honest."

"Yeah, maybe so, but . . ."

Jim's words were interrupted by the sound of hoofbeats.

His hand instinctively flew to the gun on his hip, and brought it up faster than the strike of a rattlesnake.

"What the devil is this?" Jim asked, relaxing enough to holster his six-gun.

Darby saw the Colt leap into the young man's fist, then saw his wide shoulders slump as he relaxed and holstered the gun. But rather than marvel at the fellow's gunspeed, Darby was momentarily transfixed by the extraordinary resemblance he saw between Dolly, Tracy and her long lost brother.

"Tracy," he said, turning sideways in his saddle to face her, "you are about to meet your twin brother."

"My gosh!"

What happened next was worth remembering. Tracy whipped her horse into a run and dismounted before the animal even stopped. Before Jim knew what was happening, the girl let out a whoop of joy, shouted "Howdy, brother!" and threw herself into his arms, hugging him, laughing and weeping.

Jim leaned back and studied her for a moment, then shook his head and crushed Tracy in his arms. "Well, I'll be damned," he said loud enough for everyone to hear, "I got me a sister!"

The next few hours were unforgettable. Darby just sat back and listened to the twins as they caught up on each other's lives. What was apparent was that they had been separated so young that neither remembered the other and yet . . . both had often been aware of a vague sense of loss, of being less than whole, as if they had lost something vital to their well-being.

Darby, Austin and Bert were all plenty eager to fill in the missing pieces of the twins' tragic and mysterious backgrounds. Bert especially was the one who could tell them about their infancy on the Rocking T Ranch.

"It wasn't long after you were both walking that Ginger left the ranch, weepin' and cussin'. The very next day, you were bundled up and the Hortons drove you away. And that's the last I ever saw either of you again until now."

"I don't understand it, even after it's been explained," Jim said. "Why would he send his own kids away?"

They could hear the anger and pain in the young man's voice. Everyone looked to Darby and he tried to frame an answer.

"Jim, I don't know that one person can ever understand the workings of another's mind. Judging from what I saw, your father is a very twisted man, twisted by hate, power and greed. And I suppose that he might also be the kind who refuses to face up to past mistakes. He turned on Dolly, then on you and Tracy."

Darby shook his head, bewildered. "Who can say exactly why? Perhaps he always intended to start another family and he didn't want the waters of his inheritance muddied by the children of a marriage gone bad."

"I would say that is probably true," Austin commented. "However, my personal theory is that Jim Talbot is one of those men who cannot face his own mortality. He saw his father—who he probably considered indestructible—get ambushed and die. Maybe that was when something cracked in his mind."

Tracy's twin brother shook his head. "This is all pretty wild stuff you people are tossing around. As for me, it's simple. He didn't want any part of us and I don't want any part of him—or our mother."

"Jim!" Tracy cried. "How can you say that after what you've just heard? It wasn't our mother's fault! She's been trying to find us all these years and she would have if it hadn't been for our father."

Estella took his hand. "Be forgiving. Don't harden your heart against your own mother. At least see her and let her tell you—in her own words—what really happened after you were born."

"She's right," Darby said. "Your mother risked everything to find you this one last time."

"If everything I've heard today is true," Jim said, "my father deserves nothing less than a bullet."

"Do that," Austin said, "and you'll regret it to your dying day."

"How the hell would you know about anything!" Jim demanded. "You're not much older than I am and you're just an Eastern dandy."

Austin sprang at the man and his fist connected solidly. Jim staggered, then balled his fists and came wading in with haymakers. It was immediately clear that Jim was much the stronger, but Austin was beating him to the punch, rocking him with stinging blows that peppered his face.

Jim finally caught Austin with a looping overhand so jolting that it made even Darby wince. Austin's knees buckled and he fell.

Jim stepped back, his nose dripping blood. "You had enough?"

"Hell, no!" Austin said, shaking his head to clear his vision as he struggled to his feet.

But before Austin could raise his fists, Darby stepped between the pair and kept them separated with his outstretched arms. "All right!" he bellowed. "We've got troubles enough in Whiskey Creek without both of you beating each other senseless."

Estella grabbed Jim and Tracy held Austin back, glaring at her brother. "You big bully!"

Bert slapped his knee. "Hot damn!" he hooted. "Darby, if we was to let all four of 'em tangle, wouldn't that be somethin' to watch! Better than a bag of fightin' badgers!"

"The fighting is yet to come," Darby said in a grim voice. "Two of the Rocking T gunmen have already tried to kill us. Doesn't that suggest that we will be received at that ranch with less than open arms?"

"You think my father would really try to kill us?" Jim asked, his gaze swinging from Estella to his sister.

"I'm sure of it," Darby said.

Austin rubbed his bruised knuckles. A mouse was already beginning to rise under his left eye but Jim's face looked even worse because of Austin's bony knuckles.

"If it weren't for Dolly," Darby said, "I'd be inclined to forget about that ranch."

But Jim shook his head. "If my father has done what you say, then I want to hear him admit it personally. After that, the rest of you can step aside because it's my place to settle the score."

Darby looked at Austin, who shook his head and turned away. No one doubted that Jim meant what he said and could handle a six-gun. The hotheaded fool was determined either to kill his father or to be killed by him. Either way, that would be a wrong that nothing could ever make right.

The Derby Man remembered that he'd promised to find a lawyer who would finally free Dolly from her unholy marriage. That wasn't going to be necessary now. Rather than a lawyer, they would need a coroner.

SEVENTEEN

DOLLY STARED OUT of her upstairs bedroom window at the starry Wyoming heavens. She could not sleep and had paced restlessly for hours, certain that something had gone wrong for Darby and Austin. Otherwise, they would have returned to the Rocking T for her by now.

"I have to get out of here and find them," she repeated over and over again to herself. "I can't stay here any longer. I have to go!"

For the past week, this obsession to escape had been growing stronger and stronger in her mind. She had promised Darby she would wait, but the thought that he might be hurt—or worse—was driving her insane. She couldn't eat or sleep.

Her decision finally made, Dolly rushed to her closet and dressed in a riding habit, boots and a warm coat. Her plan of escape was quite simply to tiptoe downstairs, exit through the back door and then circle around behind the shed and corrals where she'd steal a horse and ride off to Whiskey Creek. She remembered a few childhood friends who would hide and protect her until the next train passed through town, hopefully in the direction of Cheyenne where she could pick up Darby's trail.

Dolly's heart was slamming against her ribs when she paused at the door and took one last look at her room, wondering if there was anything important that she had forgotten. There wasn't. She had arrived with little more than the foolish hope that Jim would tell her where her children were to be found and at last agree to a divorce. He'd done neither and never would. Her pleas had only stiffened his resolve to keep her as his wife, if for no other reason than that it still caused her heartache.

Dolly took a deep breath and opened the door. She stepped out into the dark hallway and then tiptoed to the stairs and started down. If there was a sentry waiting below, she was going to be in even more trouble than she was already.

She was doing fine until, about halfway down the stairs, she tripped over a fishing line attached to a tin can of rocks. The can rattled wildly and Dolly was so startled that she lost her balance and almost tumbled down the stairs. Before she could recover her balance, Jim was standing on the upstairs landing holding a candle. He looked down his nose at her with contempt and maybe even some pity.

"Going somewhere, my dear?"

Dolly gulped. "Yes. I'm leaving."

"Like hell you are."

"You can't keep me a prisoner!"

"Of course I can," he said with cold amusement. "You're still my lawful wife. I can do any damned thing that I want."

"You used to get drunk and beat me."

"I still get drunk and I'll still beat you if you disobey or try to deceive me."

Dolly took a faltering step back as he started down the stairs with a dangerous look in his eyes.

He said, "This just proves that you can't be trusted and you'll have to sleep with me from now on. Maybe I won't beat you if you treat me like you did when we were first married."

Dolly began to shiver uncontrollably. "Stay away from me, Jim!"

She started to turn but he lunged to grab her. She

clawed at the flesh under his eyes, feeling it peel and fill the cavities under her nails. He yelped in pain. Bloody furrows sprang to his cheeks and leaked down his neck onto his bare chest. He dropped the candle and the stairwell was plunged back into darkness. Dolly tried to twist around and fly down the stairs but his fingers caught in her hair and he jerked her toward him so hard she felt as if he had almost broken her neck.

Dolly knew that she was in a fight for her life. She had violated his greatest vanity, his face, and now he would either kill her or degrade her without mercy. He choked and smashed at her with his big fists.

She bit him, wrenching her head sideways and ripping with her teeth until he screamed and they both lost their balance. Dolly grabbed for the bannister but it wasn't there. She fell, grunted with pain when her body struck the stairs, then momentarily lost consciousness as they both spilled down into the hallway.

For several moments Dolly lay frozen in the absolute darkness, hearing him breathe and expecting him to dig his fingers into her body and either kill or ravage her. But he did nothing. Gradually, Dolly felt her terror subside. She sat up, blinking blindly. She could hear his breathing very close and she suddenly realized that he was unconscious, perhaps even badly injured in the fall.

Dolly swayed to her feet. She staggered down the hall and through the back door, spilling off the steps and landing hard in the dirt.

"Get ahold of yourself!" she pleaded. "Use your head!"

She clenched her fists at her breast and refocused on her original plan. Feeling unsteady, she circled around the yard to the corrals. A horse, sensing her and perhaps even smelling fresh blood, snorted nervously and danced away in the starlight. Dolly gripped the corral pole. She had spent countless hours studying these cowponies in order to choose the best one, should she ever have this chance to escape. Now was her chance.

Dolly went into the tackroom and fumbled along the wall until she felt the cold steel of a bit. She pulled it and the headstall and reins free, then tossed them outside. Now a saddle. Any saddle.

Dolly had never considered herself an expert horsewoman, but she was a far better rider than the Derby Man and, within five minutes, she had caught, bridled and then saddled a handsome black mare with a blaze on her face and two stocking feet. You can adjust the stirrups later, she told herself as she mounted the mare and resisted an almost overpowering urge to kick it into a gallop that would carry her swiftly south toward Whiskey Creek.

Dolly had a bad moment when Jim's ranch dog came trotting out just as she was riding off, but she murmured its name and the dog wagged its tail and then vanished into the night. Dolly rode a hundred yards at a walk and then she whipped the mare into an easy gallop that would be sustainable for at least five miles.

Her spirit took wing! Now all she needed was friends, luck and a Union Pacific train that would carry her safely to Darby's powerful arms.

When a disheveled Dolly finally arrived in Whiskey Creek, she raised more than a few eyebrows. The very first thing she did was to gallop over to the train station, tie her exhausted mare to the hitching rail and inquire about the first train passing through Whiskey Creek in either direction.

"One comes through tomorrow morning," the ticketmaster said.

"Heading east or west?"

"West."

"Damn!" Dolly swore. "When is the next one leaving for Cheyenne?"

"In four days."

"I can't wait that long," Dolly said anxiously. "There

used to be a Miss Shirley Robinson who lived in this town. Do you know her?"

"I know everyone. That girl got married and moved away years ago."

Dolly pulled another name from her list of childhood friends. "What about . . . Cindy Atwood? Big girl with buck teeth and freckles?"

"Gone, too. She fell in with a gambling man and they left with the construction crews last year."

Dolly's spirits plummeted. "Thanks," she said, turning and walking away, trying to decide what to do next. By the time she reached her horse, Dolly knew that she could not wait even a single day for the westbound train, not if she expected to escape the grasp of her ruthless, insane husband.

Dolly remounted her mare and rode down to Whiskey Creek's only general store. She didn't recognize the proprietor, a weary-looking man in his fifties with a nervous, birdlike wife.

"I need to buy a used six-gun and a few provisions," she told them.

The wife peered out the door. "Ain't that a Rockin' T horse you're ridin'?"

"Why, yes. That's where I come from," Dolly said, "but I'm afraid that I don't have any cash. I left rather suddenly and forgot it."

The pair exchanged skeptical glances. The man said, "Without money, we can't help you, ma'am. This is a business, not a charity."

"I understand. But what if I trade you my saddle and blanket? That ought to be at least worth an old percussion revolver and a little food."

"Sorry," the woman snapped. "That bein' a Rockin' T outfit you're ridin', we ain't about to cross Mr. Talbot."

"That's right," her husband said. "Are you Mrs. Talbot?"

"Sure she is!" the woman carped. "Walt, are you going blind?"

Dolly could see that there was no point in carrying on this discussion. No doubt everyone in Whiskey Creek was either beholden to or afraid of Jim Talbot. They would do nothing to risk their lives or their businesses.

"Good day," she said, hurrying back outside, angry at herself for not thinking to bring some cash.

With the whole town watching, Dolly climbed wearily back on her exhausted mare. If she remembered correctly, she would ride past an old apple orchard just east of town. If the apples were in season and weren't all picked, she could fill her saddlebags and survive the ride to Cheyenne. Once there, Dolly was certain that she could sell the good Rocking T mare and her saddle, then take a stage down to Denver. It would be hopscotch, one jump ahead of her crazed husband, but what other choice did she have?

Dolly galloped west out of Whiskey Creek. However, the moment she was out of sight, she looped back around and headed east down toward Cheyenne. Maybe this little ruse would give her a few hours of extra breathing room to get away from those who would already be on her trail, but she seriously doubted it. It was another fifty miles to Cheyenne, but once she got over the summit just ahead, it was all downhill.

EIGHTEEN

THE DERBY MAN guessed that it was about two o'clock in the afternoon and they were a good twenty miles west of Cheyenne when they observed someone leading a lame horse down the eastern slope of the Laramie Mountains. When they drew closer, Darby saw a mass of golden hair, a familiar smile and a figure that could belong to none other than the woman he loved.

"That's my Dolly!" he shouted, forcing Hallelujah into a gallop.

Darby was not graceful when he piled off the preacher's horse but Dolly didn't notice or care. With a screech of pure joy, she dropped the reins of her lame mare and threw herself into Darby's open arms with such force they both crashed over backward.

"How did you escape!"

"It wasn't easy," Dolly confessed. Her smile faded and she cast a worried look back toward the mountains. "Darby, he's coming."

"Good!" Darby exclaimed. "There will be no more running or hiding. We'll settle this once and for all."

"But . . ." Whatever objections Dolly had were instantly forgotten when she saw her children. She blinked as if not trusting her own eyes. "Darby," she breathed, "are these . . ."

"Yes," he said, stepping aside.

For a moment, everyone was mute, but then Tracy broke the spell and cried, "Mother!" as she threw herself from her horse.

Darby felt his eyes sting as mother and daughter were finally reunited. They were a lovely pair to watch under Wyoming's immense blue skies as they hugged and cried until even old Bert was sniffling.

Tears were pouring down Estella's cheeks and she whispered, "Jim, say hello to your mother."

He stepped down from his horse, a tall, powerful young man with a square jaw, broad shoulders, curly blond hair and a very battered face, thanks to Austin.

"Howdy," he said, removing his hat and shuffling his boots awkwardly.

Dolly gazed up at her son. "Howdy, yourself." She gently touched a purple welt under his right eye. "My, but someone has given you a nasty beating. It wasn't my Derby Man, was it?"

He grinned a little lopsidedly. "Naw, it was that skinny dude yonder on the horse. But I was just warmin' up when Darby saved him. Ma, I'd like you to meet the girl I'm fixin' to marry. This here is Miss Estella Flynn."

Estella dismounted and extended her hand. "I am so happy to meet you."

Dolly shook the girl's hand and blinked wetly. "I guess we all have a lot of catching up to do if—if we survive my crazy husband. Darby, maybe we should turn around and run for Cheyenne. There's no telling how many guns Jim will bring over from the Rocking T Ranch."

Darby's eyes followed the road east, paralleling the railroad tracks. "Any idea how far behind they are?"

"About noon, I saw the flash of metal against the mountainside, probably one of those silver conchos he keeps shined up on his bridle. He's close."

Jim pulled out his six-gun and spun the cylinder. Quickly remounting his horse, he said, "What happens next is between me and that no-good sonofabitch!"

"Now, wait a minute!" Darby shouted.

But it was too late. The fool was already riding off at a gallop.

"Blast!"

"We can't let him face them alone," Austin said. "Son or no son, Talbot will kill him in the blink of an eyelash."

"That's right," Darby said, reaching for his saddlehorn and hauling himself back onto Hallelujah.

There was a lot of shouting from the women but neither Darby nor Austin gave them any mind as they raced to catch young Talbot. After a mile of hard galloping, Darby glanced back over his shoulder to see that Bert and the women were coming too, Dolly riding double behind Tracy.

The Derby Man gritted his teeth, thinking that they were a pretty sorry fighting force—three women, a blind broncbuster, two dudes and a young hothead far too eager to get himself shot by his own father.

Suddenly, Darby saw the Rocking T outfit materialize from behind a low, rutted ridge.

"Jim!" he shouted. "Wait!"

But young Talbot wasn't waiting for anyone. He was the best horseman on the fastest mount. Jim was still a good mile ahead of the others when he met his father and four Rocking T gunmen.

Darby yanked his shotgun from its scabbard and checked the loads. Right beside him, Austin and Bert did the same with their rifles. As he galloped on, the Derby Man could hear angry words pass between father and son and then his heart stopped when he saw both Talbots make a play for their six-guns.

Two shots split the afternoon air and blended it with gunsmoke. The son toppled from his horse and the father, swaying like a drunk, hooked spurs into his horse's flanks, causing it to bolt and race back toward the Laramie Mountains.

The four hired gunmen milled about for a moment in

confusion, uncertain of what to do, until one of them wheeled his horse around and galloped after their employer. The others glanced over at Darby, Austin and Bert, then followed suit.

Austin was the first to reach young Jim but Darby was only a few seconds behind, followed by Bert. From behind them came the sound of Estella's anguished cry as she drew near enough to realize that the man she loved had been shot.

Jim's eyes fluttered open and his lips pulled back in a grimace of pain. "Tell Estella to quit that damned hollerin'. I'm still going to marry her."

"Good," Darby said, feeling a wave of relief. He watched as Austin pressed a monogrammed silk handkerchief to Jim's side, staunching the flow of blood. "Just rest easy."

Darby came to his feet. He could see that Jim's father had toppled from his horse. His hired gunmen were gathered around him.

"I'm going to make sure this is finished," Darby said, remounting.

"Wait!" Austin called.

Darby, however, wasn't in a mood to wait. He rode forward with his shotgun cocked and ready but was quickly joined by Austin and Bert, though the old man was actually a liability if shooting erupted.

"Throw down your weapons!" Darby bellowed as they drew near.

"Mr. Talbot's a goner!" one of the gunmen called. "We're out of this fracas now—dead men don't make their payrolls."

"You're also finished at the Rocking T!" Austin shouted, lifting his rifle to his shoulder. "Ride and don't even stop in Whiskey Creek!"

"Why the hell not? Listen . . ."

Bert cursed and fired his rifle. His shot sailed a good thirty feet over the gunmen's heads but it was enough to send them racing away. Startled, Hallelujah lowered his head and began to buck. Darby dropped his reins and held on to his saddlehorn until Austin could ride up and grab the bridle.

"Damn you, Bert!" Darby shouted in anger. "Next time you open fire, give me a warning!"

Bert's cheeks reddened. "If you ever learned to ride, you wouldn't need a warning!"

Darby tumbled off Hallelujah and went over to kneel beside Talbot, wanting to ask the rancher why he'd made life so miserable for Dolly and his children. But the man was already dead.

"To hell with it," Darby muttered to himself as he trudged back toward the women, "maybe he was just plain mean to the bone."

When Dolly rushed into his arms and hugged his neck, Darby said, "Talbot is dead. It's finally over."

Dolly sniffled and then kissed his mouth. She looked back at her wounded son and pretty daughter. "Derby, honey, just this once, you're wrong."

"Huh?"

"It's not over—it's just beginning."

The Derby Man smiled and reached for a Cuban cigar, because Dolly was right.

ABOUT THE AUTHOR

GARY McCARTHY is the author of the Darby Buckingham novels published in the Double D Western line, along with many other Western and historical novels. His most recent Double D Western is *The Gringo Amigo*. He lives in Ojai, California.

FIC
MCCAR

McCarthy, Gary.

Whiskey Creek.